Table of C

CW00584697

Al Clark

by Jonathan G. Meyer

AL CLARK

Copyright

Dedicated to my family,
For which, if not for them,
I would be nothing.

AL CLARK

Standing at the top of a grass-covered hill, with a sweet smelling breeze at his back, he reveled in the bright morning sunshine of a perfect spring day. Jagged heights filled the horizon as the sun hoisted itself up and kissed the mountain tops.

In the valley below, a small idyllic village was shaking off the night and was well into the process of beginning a new day. The faraway villagers appeared to be enjoying the day as much as he.

Someone was running up the hill towards him, yelling something—a couple of words over and over; maybe a name, maybe a warning? He cupped his ears with his hands to better hear what the person was saying, but the sounds came muffled and distorted; carried away by the wind.

The person got closer and closer, arms and legs pumping, and the words began to get clearer until just on the verge of understanding, the scene turned a blinding white and then quickly—faded to black.

Chapter One

He awoke gradually, a little at a time, swimming up from the abyss.

His eyes opened to near total darkness, and all he saw was a small spot of light directly overhead. A tiny star surrounded by a velvety darkness. A single bright dot in the void that grew and expanded to fill his vision until he blinked, and it returned to a tiny pinhole of light.

He could see just enough to determine he was lying in a box not much larger than his body. The soft glow from the pinhole over his head allowed just enough light to see cold dark metal surrounding him. Somewhere far away an alarm was sounding. His head swung back and forth frantically trying to understand, and fear grabbed at his heart as a disturbing realization surfaced. *Where am I?*

Desperately he raised his arms and pressed hard on the surface above him. He felt a slight shift to his right, so he concentrated his efforts on that side. His fear made him strong, and with surprising speed the lid flew open on concealed hinges and bounced off something—only to slam closed again. For part of a second, he managed a glimpse of a small gray room and an oval metal door just a few feet beyond the end of the box.

A second attempt to free himself, using less effort, was rewarded with the lid swinging to the side and remaining open. The distant alarm outside the metal box changed to a loud screech as the man eased himself into a sitting position and tried to make sense of his surroundings.

It was a small and utilitarian room, a cubby hole with barely enough room for the silver metal box. The lighting was minimal, leaving details fuzzy, but it appeared this room was designed specifically for the box. Behind him, a control panel with insistent flashing lights and that annoying alarm blared on the back wall.

His eyes began to adjust to the low-level lighting and allowed a closer look at the unfamiliar place he found himself. The box was in the center of the room with barely five feet of space surrounding it. A dull gray color dominated.

The annoying alarm fed his dull throbbing headache and was quickly turning it into a raging pain in his head. He reached around and inspected the control panel. To one side was a switch marked ALARM RESET. He reached up and pressed it, and the room fell into silence. That was much better. Now he could think.

The room was unadorned. The door, the control panel, and a small pair of cabinet doors on the wall opposite of the steps were the only features. On the side of the box there appeared to be lettering. Unfortunately, the letters were faded to the point of being unreadable.

His attire consisted of an off-white uniform of some kind, with long sleeves, creased trousers, and small golden buttons. A pair of black deck boots completed the outfit that could be considered military, or maybe medical. The clothing was not in the least familiar to him. He checked his pockets one by one, and found them empty, with no clues leading to answers.

Waking in a box, disoriented and confused, not knowing where you were or how you came to be there—is the stuff of nightmares. None of this made sense. He stared at the door, puzzling over where *here* was and had a revelation that took this bad dream to a whole new level. Try as he might, he could not recall his name. *Who am I?*

He struggled to remember anything about himself and came up with nothing. The memories were just not there.

The man climbed out of the box and found three small steps leading to the floor. Out of the bottom of the box, several dull colored pipes could be seen disappearing into the floor. He wondered if the box was some form of life support system.

The sound of his boots echoed in the small space when he stepped over to puzzle over the small cabinet doors. There was a keypad to the right of the doors beside a glowing red indicator light. He punched in a few numbers, but nothing happened. The doors were locked and would not open without the proper code.

He turned and stood in front of the oval hatch that served as a door, and triggered a sensor, causing it to slide silently into the wall. When the door opened, a slight breath of fresh air blew past his face. He stepped over the threshold and looked left, and then right, to discover a long, empty corridor going both ways, dimly lit, and circling slightly upward out of sight. Ten feet tall and ten feet wide with a curved ceiling, the passageway had six-foot portals placed on both sides every fifteen or twenty feet.

The corridor and doors were a neutral gray color, with a faded orange stripe above the doors on both sides; now dull and without luster. His guess attributed the striping to an indication of sections or areas.

Next to each entrance were faded peeling letters, such as LQ26...LQ27, with even numbers on the left and odd numbers to the right. He turned around and looked closely at the lettering on the door he just came through. It was barely readable, and appeared to be Albert, or Alvin maybe; Al—something—Clark, with the number 25 below it.

If this is Al Clark's room, does that mean I am Al Clark?

He decided that going left was as good as going right, so he moved to the first door to his left, marked LQ26, and pressed a small button on the right side of the hatch. The barrier slid silently into the wall revealing a dark room. As he walked inside, there was a soft 'click,' and hidden lighting lit up a room much larger than the one he just left; although there was no wasted space. The room was tinted a faded yellow with a curved ceiling that started above the door and arced down to end at the far wall.

The presence of a door inside told him there was more than one room. In the first room was a double bed, a table, and a small desk with a computer terminal mounted on the wall above it. He crossed to the terminal thinking it might help with his questions, but pressing the ON button had no effect. In the center of the simple room stood a multi-purpose round table and two chairs locked in notches to the floor.

The other room was a complete bathroom with a stand-up shower, a small sink, and a toilet. The apartment had everything one might need to fill the basic requirements of a couple. With a few modifications, maybe a small family. Both rooms were empty, with no sign of personal belongings or previous occupation. It looked as if these rooms had been unoccupied for many years, with no brightness to the color, and no shiny surfaces to reflect the light.

Above the sink in the bathroom was a clouded metal mirror that showed the reflection of a man in his early forties, six foot tall, with short brown hair and haunted blue eyes. It was an ordinary looking stranger's reflection that did nothing to tell him his identity. He didn't remember hitting his head, but there was a tiny drop of dried blood in the middle of his forehead. He wiped it away with his hand.

A little overwhelmed, he went back to the main room and sat down on the bed to think. These accommodations did not look worn; these rooms looked unused and old. No scuffed corners or marks of wear on the floor. There were no papers that littered the room; no books on the desk, no bedding covered the bed, and the bathroom appeared old and never used. These living quarters were all ready to move into and never occupied. *Why build all this, and never use it?* A short time later, he got up and returned to the corridor. He left the room and was standing outside when there was a soft *'click,'* the overhead lighting returned to its long held off state, and the door closed automatically. He wondered, *Where are all the people?*

He made his way down the passageway, tripping the lighting into other rooms and found similar quarters; each tinted a different soft color. Some had three rooms, but all were empty and forgotten. Eventually, he found himself at a large hatch blocking any further travel down the corridor.

Beside the door, a large sign declared: ACCESS TO BLUE SECTION and SPOKE 4 LIFT. Directly below the sign was a small control panel with a card reader slot and two indicator lights; a green light labeled OK TO OPEN was lit, and a red one with text that read DO NOT OPEN, was not.

In the center of the hatch was a small round window with thick plastic or glass that he wiped with his sleeve, allowing him to see into a round room about twenty feet across, with a faded ten-foot red circle painted in the center. On the far side of this transition space was an identical door and window; leading to another corridor.

The card slot told him a key card was needed to open the hatch and gain access to the space beyond. After thinking for a moment, he turned around and hurried back to end up at the other end of the corridor. This one section of the passageway, from large exit door to large exit door, was easily a thousand feet long, so it took him a few minutes to get to the opening at the other end. When he arrived, he found a key card was needed to gain access to this door also. He was trapped in this section of the passageway and had traded his small man-sized prison for a larger one; with rooms.

Now...Where in this place can I get a key card?

Thinking back, he could remember only one location where he might find an item as important as a key card. The locked cabinet in 'Al Clark's' room. He needed to return to the place where he started and attempt to access the storage compartment. It was the best option available.

Back in the room he woke up in, he stood before the keypad next to the cabinet and considered the code required to unlock the cabinet doors. It was probably four or five digits;

something memorable for the owner. Depending on what it secured, and the person that programmed it, the code could be devilishly complicated or as simple as 1234. He tapped in 1-2-3-4. That wasn't it. He tried 1-1-1-1. Not it either. He attempted several different combinations, and none of them worked.

The only thing he knew for certain about this place was the lettering on the door: *Al—Clark-25. If A = 1, and C = 3, if you added twenty-five to the end, the combination would be 1-3-2-5.* To his amazement, when he tried this solution there was a faint 'click,' and the two cabinet doors popped open. A small smile crept onto his face as he opened the doors, and he thought, *I would never have bet on that to work.*

Inside, there was the key card he needed; complete with a cord to hang around his neck, a small set of old-fashioned looking keys, and a handgun in a holster. He reached up and took down the weapon. When he wrapped his hand around the grip, it felt comfortable and familiar in his hand.

Slowly, pieces began to come back to him. A puzzle of fragmented thoughts pulled themselves together, and he realized that he knew what this weapon was. It was a modulated laser pistol, commonly referred to as an MLP.

With this, someone could blow tiny holes in anything that wasn't hardened metal. Mostly for security, it was the weapon of choice for air-tight facilities—and he knew how to use it.

Still smiling, he hung the card around his neck and put the keys in his pants pocket. The pistol's power pack was depleted and needed recharging, but he clipped it to his belt thinking there must be somewhere around here where it could be charged, or the power pack replaced.

He had no idea who he was, or where he was, and believed the card would help lead him to some understanding. The small plastic rectangle could very well be his ticket to the answers he so deeply needed.

Chapter Two

H e exited the room, turned left, and walked back down the corridor to the hatch that required a key card. Along the way, he pulled the little plastic rectangle from his pocket and took a closer look at it. On one side was emblazoned a single word *Excalibur*. On the back was a place for a name. However, it was not filled in. Seemingly random letters and numbers filled out the bottom. The card was a generic card that could be programmed to allow the recipient access to specific areas, except this recipient had not bothered to fill in the name. Efficient and nonproprietary, this access card provided few clues.

The card worked, though, and it opened the hatch into the room at the end of the corridor separating the two passageways. Once inside, he noticed a similar control panel on the inside of each hatch and another in-between the two doors. The openings had faded signs stating: ACCESS TO ORANGE SECTION, and ACCESS TO BLUE SECTION. The central control panel sign was labeled: SPOKE 4 LIFT. The doors leading to the passageway had the accompanying safety lights, indicating if the door was safe to open.

He passed on through what he was beginning to believe was an airlock, into the other passageway and found it very similar to the one he just left; except the stripe above the doors was a soft blue. Most doors were labeled LQ...something, with the numbers increasing as he went down the corridor. A few doors were labeled UTILITY, which usually contained cleaning supplies and assorted equipment. When he came to a door marked MESS HALL, he grinned. Almost everyone knew what a MESS Hall was—food! He walked in, and the door closed silently behind him.

It was a fairly large room, and designed for food consumption, with room for seventy-five to a hundred people to eat at the same time. All along one side was a counter with recesses to display a variety of foods. In a back storage area, he found sealed boxes full of various packaged meals, and a user-friendly device for heating the pre-made packets. He warmed one at random, and quickly opened it; squeezing the food labeled Meatloaf and Potatoes into his mouth. The taste was bland. Still, it helped him to feel better.

The water from the tap behind the counter ran a little grayish for a minute or so until it turned relatively clear. He stuck his head under the faucet and sipped from the bottom of the tap. The tepid drink tasted a little like metal but quenched his thirst.

The water must be a closed system and continually recycled.

With his need for food and water satisfied, the man moved out of the mess hall and headed towards the door at the end of the corridor. He would remember this place: Blue Section = Food.

He continued his explorations until he reached the end of the blue section. Again, there was the transition room between the corridors. The inside of this chamber was identical to the one between the orange and blue sections. In this case, it was an airlock for access to the blue section, the green section, and spoke lift three.

The hatch to the green corridor did not display a green light. On the control panel was a bright glowing red light that warned—DO NOT OPEN. Through the round window of the hatch leading to the green corridor, the reason for the ominous crimson light became apparent. Beyond the sealed barrier a large section of the passageway was missing, leaving the passage beyond open to space. The corridor had a hole passing through it; where stars were visible.

The stars told him he was in space, possibly in the centrifugal gravity ring of a space station, or a large ship. It did not matter that the passageway lights were out beyond the window, the starlight told him all he needed to know. Thirty feet past the door was a large ragged hole through the center of the corridor. There was no going beyond this point without a space suit. Now he wondered just how many sections were damaged.

Was this place abandoned for a reason?

He returned to the orange corridor, back to where his day started and contemplated what he knew. He had awakened in a box in a room labeled Al...*something*...Clark. His clothing consisted of a uniform, and somehow he knew how to use an MLP handgun. The station seemed empty of people, appeared old, but at the same time unused. The ring must still be rotating, or he wouldn't have gravity. There was food and water in the mess hall for a large number of people, and in the areas he had been through, there was living space for at least two-hundred people. To add to the mystery, he had not found a single working computer.

It took him almost an hour to get to the end of the orange corridor. He took his time and investigated areas he had run by before and noticed several places he'd missed in his rush to get information. There were several doors marked UTILITY, and some keyed doors marked MAINTENANCE. His card worked on these doors also, and inside he found electrical equipment, HVAC equipment. A few had workstations with tools neatly displayed and secured.

In the orange section, he found a security office, with several interconnected rooms and even a holding cell; waiting for its first jailbird. On a long table in a back room, he discovered a place to charge the power pack for his pistol.

From a line of fully charged cells, he swapped the dead battery pack in the weapon for a charged pack and watched as the power indicator went from red to green, indicating a full charge. He checked the safety and pushed the switch from red to green, placing it in the safe mode. Being armed, for some reason, was reassuring.

His card had not failed to open any doors except the one that would put him in a corridor open to space. He did not even *try* his card on that door.

When he finally reached the airlock at the other end of the orange section, he went through to the passage marked YELLOW SECTION. Nearly identical to the other passageways, he followed it to the next airlock and found that insistent red light on the panel leading into the green part of the ring.

Okay, there are four parts to the ring: orange, blue, green, and yellow. Only the green section was open to space. That would mean there must be four 'spokes.' It was time to see where the spoke lifts would take him.

****

HIS EXPLORATIONS WERE beginning to wear on him. It had been a long day, but he was determined to get as much information as he could before he slept. He didn't like the idea of trying to access a spoke lift when one of the doors showed a glowing red light, so he returned to the airlock between the yellow and orange section that was red light free.

The center control panel was labeled: ACCESS TO SPOKE 4, and on it was the standard red and green indicator lights. Below the control panel, bold lettering cautioned, STAND OUTSIDE RED CIRCLE. He was standing outside the circle. Still, he hesitated for a second before sliding the card through the slot. Somewhere above him came a series of *thunks*, and in the center of the ceiling two halves of a circle retracted to open a passage.

Through this hole in the ceiling descended what looked like a large capsule. A conveyance like no transport capsule he'd ever seen before. Although he could tell it was old by its dull coloring and cloudy windows, it was still a thing of beauty. Twelve feet tall and eight feet around, it was smooth and streamlined. A triumph of technology. The entire middle section was clear plastic, except for a man-sized access door.

He cautiously stepped into the capsule, and the interior lights *'clicked'* on. The inside of the compartment was empty, except for the simple controller on the wall with a button for the door and a card slot to activate the lift.

In the center of the capsule—was a tree. Four inches around and topped with four short branches at shoulder height. Age had turned it a dull green, with yellow highlights that created what some might call sculpture in a stark environment.

He wondered, *is it form or is it function?*

The door closed automatically as soon as he used the card and a dull vibration could be felt through the floor as the capsule started slowly rising, gaining speed as it went. The pale silver walls of the spoke slid rapidly by, and as the capsule shot up, he noticed his card beginning to float from his chest. He had an idea of what was coming next, so he grabbed for the tree.

This feeling was something he knew. It seemed he was familiar with zero gravity. The tree was the perfect handhold to keep him from floating around and causing himself harm. *Functional as well as beautiful.*

The ride to this point had been smooth and silent, but as he approached the top of the spoke, and the lift started slowing down, the vibration intensified as if it were struggling. He was just beginning to worry when the capsule slid out of the spoke and ground to a halt—into nothing.

His eyes gradually adjusted, and he spied far away lights slowly moving in the distance; both in front and behind. To his side were stationary lights similar to the other beacons. A door closed below him and allowed the distant lights to appear more distinct. When his eyes adjusted he could see well enough to determine his whereabouts.

He appeared to be inside a giant metal ball, as seen from the inside, easily one hundred feet across. The lights he saw were the indicator lights of the other spoke lifts as they rotated slowly around. On each side, the vague outline of two stationary doors beckoned.

To delay his search did not enter his mind. It was now time to get some answers. With one hand holding the tree, he reached out and pressed the button to open the door. Bright lighting quickly ramped up outside the capsule until he could see the immense open space at the center of the huge wheel. The *Hub* of the ring. He floated out of the capsule and turned, to find a boy hanging onto a recessed handle; just floating there with wide open eyes staring straight at him.

Chapter Three

The boy made no effort to move, and the look on his face was one of complete surprise. His voice squeaked a little at first until he finally forced out, "Are you...real?"

The man laughed and shook his head. He said, "Are you?"

The young man was relatively clean, with blue coveralls, long blonde hair, brown eyes, and a *big* smile. He was around eighteen, and maybe a little taller than the man.

The boy told him, "My hibernation pod malfunctioned almost a year ago, and I've been waiting for someone to show up ever since. I can't tell you how glad I am to see you. I'm Christopher Morris...who are you?"

"Well, for the time being, I guess you can call me Al."

"Umm, Al...what?"

"Clark...Al Clark." He looked down, chuckled and said, "It's a long story, Christopher. For now, how about you tell me about yourself."

Christopher was lonely and talkative. He suggested they go to the quarters he was using in the yellow section to sit down and talk. Al pushed off and floated towards the capsule he rode up in when the young man stopped him.

"I wouldn't use that lift if I were you—it doesn't sound right. I use the number one lift. Two and three won't work because the doors are overridden and locked, so one is the only lift that works as it should."

Al considered the vibration he felt on his way up, and decided he didn't like the number four capsule either.

The boy chose one of the larger living quarters with three rooms, close to the number one spoke because he liked hanging out in the zero gravity of the hub; to help him relax, he said. He wasn't worried about housekeeping in his quarters, and it showed, to the point where Al had to move some things to sit across from him at the small table. The boy offered him an energy bar to which he declined, and they began talking.

The biggest question on Al's mind was, "Where are we, Christopher?"

"Please, call me Chris, and right now we are in a habitat ring located on the front of a spaceship called the *Excalibur*. You don't know where you are?"

"I figured out I was in space, and on what seems to be an abandoned space ship or a space station. What I don't know—is where. Let me ask you this. Do I look familiar to you? I mean, have you seen me before?"

Chris took a close look at Al and replied, "You don't look familiar, but they rushed me onto the ship at the last minute, and I didn't meet many people."

Al's disappointment was evident. He took a deep breath and said, "Okay, I guess I need to explain why it is I'm so clueless."

He told Chris about waking up in the box, not knowing where or who he was, and about his excursions so far, up until the time he found Chris staring back at him across the hub.

When Al finished, Chris told his story about how he was thrown out of his hibernation pod to an empty habitat ring. For the better part of a year, he had almost gone crazy living by himself and trying to stay busy. A seemingly endless number of long days and longer nights. He now knew the ship like the back of his hand and spent extended periods of time exploring.

Chris jumped up and grabbed something from the bed and gave it to Al. "I started a journal. I missed the first two days and made an entry every day since."

Al thumbed through the eight by ten notebook and found it surprisingly easy to read, complete with intricate drawings covering a broad spectrum of subjects. A map of the interior of the habitat ring was laid out in detail. "These sketches are good Chris. I am impressed."

"What else did I have to do? Some of those drawings took up weeks of my time," the boy joked.

Chris described the room where he awoke, and Al thought it sounded a lot like the cubicle that held his coffin-like box.

Chris was told there were a thousand people aboard the Excalibur. He admitted he didn't know for sure, as he had been rushed in to fill a last minute cancellation, and had seen little of the ship. He believed the person he replaced must have died before he could get aboard the starship because the lottery they held included hundreds-of-thousands of applicants from all over the Earth. If you had a hundred dollars and could pass the strict physical and psychological tests, you had a chance. Finally, one-thousand people were picked by the Excalibur committee to be aboard the ship when it left. The lucky ones.

The Earth had become a difficult place to live; due to runaway global climate change and its effects. There were wars all over the planet making it seem like half the world was always fighting someone for something. Many people wanted to go to a place like the planets described in the lottery brochures.

Chris had a limited access card that didn't work all the doors. Because of the limited access, he was unable to get past the hub to the rest of the ship. He was trapped in the giant wheel and spent his time exploring the habitat ring when he wasn't relaxing in the ring's center because of the zero-gravity.

He was in the hub when the meteor shower took out the green section just two days ago, and it almost scared him to death. He told Al the ring could handle small rocks because it was self-healing, but the big ones were unstoppable and made a racket inside the ship that is unimaginable.

Al sat back and thought, *Could it be the meteor shower that woke me?* His thoughts were sluggish; fragmented. If it *had* been two days since he slept, he needed to rest. Al considered whether he should move into quarters of his own, or help Chris clean this one. To simplify their future planning, he decided to help Chris. The boy was happy to oblige.

Later, with Al just about to fall asleep in one room, and Chris in the other, Al called out through the open door, "If this is a colony ship, where are we going?"

"We *were* on a thirty-year journey to a planet called Avalon."

"Thirty years, huh? To colonize?"

"Yeah, that was the plan."

****

THE NEXT MORNING, AFTER taking turns getting showers, they dressed and headed for the mess hall in the blue section. They each grabbed a food package, heated them up, and took the food to a table to eat.

Sitting and talking at one of the many empty tables, they agreed that somewhere on this ship there were people, either dead or alive. Anxious to get moving, they finished their meals and headed to the hub to find them. While they walked to the number one lift, Chris filled Al in on what he knew of the mission and their ship.

"This ship, the *Excalibur*, left earth orbit in 2160. It was decided by the 'people in charge,' that all colonists and crew would be put into hibernation until three months before the ship established orbit around the planet; to minimize resource usage. At that time the crew was to be awakened, and then a team of specialists would begin waking the scientists. Finally, the colonists would be revived. When we arrived at Avalon, we would have been ready to assess the planet, and send people down to set up housing almost right away."

None of what Chris said jogged any memories. It was like a science fiction story he'd never read.

Chris continued, "The habitat ring was to be used to house the people after revival until planetfall, and then for the subsequent operations. The ship is fully automated, and the computer was programmed to wake the crew when ready or if there was an emergency. I guess that didn't work out so well."

Something had gone wrong, and Chris and Al were either the first to wake up or the last ones alive. A forty-something amnesiac, and an eighteen-year-old kid.

Chris continued, "When they first discovered Avalon with one of the telescopes in orbit around the moon, it was considered a pretty significant find. The planet they found was in a Goldilocks orbit around its yellow sun, and the images sent back showed a world very similar to Earth. An early Earth before the industrial revolution. In other words, Earth—before we messed it up.

"They got the name Avalon from a mythical island paradise detailed in the legends of King Arthur. It was where they forged his sword *Excalibur* and where he went to recover after the battle of Camlann."

The boy laughed and told Al he had gotten all this from the brochure advertising the lottery. After reading their glorified description, he said he was hooked.

"Avalon was not the only planet reachable within a thirty-year journey. Four starships were built and sent to different promising planets. They were assembled in space in a geostationary orbit around Earth, and it took five years to build each ship. As soon as one starship was finished and launched, another was begun.

"A lottery was set up for a place on a vessel, and it raked in trillions. They charged one-hundred U.S. dollars per ticket, and the money financed the building of the ships. The rest was supposed to help those most affected by rising sea levels, catastrophic storms, species extinction and so forth. The ships turned out to be extravagantly expensive, of course, but the people attempting to save the planet still got almost half, which was a lot of money. Unfortunately, it did little to make the Earth more livable.

"Our ship, the Excalibur, was the last one built of the four. It benefited from its predecessors in that it had the best of everything. There's supposed to be a very extensive seed bank for crop promotion, a large hydroponic farm, and the latest design of primary fusion drive that money could buy. The hibernation pods had all the bugs worked out and were the best models built to date. They also said the master control computer was one hundred times better than the computer on the first ship.

"Our ship is like a modern day Titanic, with everything needed for a long voyage. Except the Titanic was for recreation, and the *Excalibur* is for survival."

Chris was the last one aboard the last ship, which means he was the last person allowed off the planet.

The two shipmates entered the capsule for the number one spoke using Chris's card. They both grabbed hold of the tree, and Al activated the lift. They watched the walls of the spoke slide by, and as they got closer to the hub, Chris began to smile. When the lift reached the top of the tube and stopped, he looked at Al and said, "Is there anything like zero gravity? I will never get tired of it."

As soon as the door opened and the lights came on, Chris pushed off and sailed gracefully to the far wall, where he grabbed a waiting handle. Like a monkey, he then swung from handle to handle spinning around the circular hub until he got back to Al, where he stopped, smiled, and said, "Ever flown before?"

"To be honest, I'm not sure...let's see."

Al pushed off to try and follow Chris's example. As it turned out, it was trickier than it looked. The lift section was slowly revolving, and they had to be careful not to bang into the raised capsule as it rotated around. In addition, if you landed on the rotating section it would change your trajectory and make you go where you didn't want to. In the end, the two spacemen proved Al was reasonably proficient, and Chris, who had spent many hours practicing in the hub, was easily deemed an expert.

Chapter Four

After a little discussion, they decided to find the bridge first. Al figured if there were working computers, they would be there, and they could gain a lot of useful information. There may also be a labeled schematic of the ship or a log book to tell them where they needed to go. Hopefully, there would be something there to give them more information.

The two hatches on both sides of the hub had clear markings. Bold lettering on one door said MAIN SHIP and the other said BRIDGE. Simple, and not very descriptive. There were the standard control panels, and both doors had green lights. Things were looking good so far.

Chris showed Al how his card wouldn't work on the bridge door, so Al tried his—and nothing happened. A second attempt also failed. He looked closer at the control panel, but it appeared to be no different than the others. Al looked at Chris and said, "Ok, that didn't work, how about we try the other door?"

The door labeled Main Ship sighed, and then slid aside after Al pulled his card through the reader. Inside the door was a smaller version of the habitat ring airlocks. After the first door had closed behind them, they walked across and opened the secondary door. What they found was the breadbasket for the ship.

Their eyes adjusted to the brightly lit room, and before them stretched a long wide aisle with planting beds on both sides going all the way to the other end, where there was another door. Row after row of ten by twenty-foot hydroponic beds, loaded with plants and separated by narrow two-foot walkways, filled both sides of the room. In the efficient beds was a bumper crop of all kinds of vegetables: corn, potatoes, squash, lettuce, melons, and further down what appeared to be herbs.

Industriously moving about them, a dozen three-foot tall robots tended the plants. Slender enough to fit through the walkways, they looked like sharp pointed bullets standing on end; with arms. Long spindly appendages that could reach anywhere in a plant bed and were raised straight up when navigating the walkways. Chris immediately nicknamed them, *Pinheads*.

The robots, busy harvesting their crops, ignored the two humans slowly walking down the central aisle. The room, maybe fifty feet tall and two hundred feet long, was a cornucopia of produce.

"This stuff has been growing for a while, what do you think activated it? Chris asked.

Al was still taking it all in, his head following the long line of planting beds. He turned to Chris and said, "I would think the growing of crops wouldn't start until just before we arrived at Avalon. Why is it here going full blast? We need to find out where this ship is, and exactly how much time has passed."

"Look—tomatoes!" Chris exclaimed. He ran the last couple steps and snatched a ripe tomato from the vine. His face lit up when he took a bite, and he said, "Best tomato ever! I've been living on packaged food so long; I almost forgot what a fresh tomato tastes like."

Towards the center of the farm, on the right side, was a chute labeled *Incinerator*. Three pinheads were loading fruits, vegetables, and plant matter into it; causing the food to disappear into the belly of the ship.

Chris asked Al, "Why do you think they are doing that?"

"No one here to eat it I guess," replied Al.

They moved on. When the two searchers reached the door at the other end of the aisle, they found it labeled with a more stylistic sign declaring it to be, *THE PARK*. Neither spoke, however both were thinking, *This sounded promising*.

Al opened the door into a large space, similar in size to the farm, only here was a perfect replica of a full grown Earth park—at night. A park complete with trees, benches, winding paths, and grass. Above them, simulated stars and a full moon filtered light throughout the park, and there was a gentle breeze circulating from somewhere that brought with it the evening scents of Earth in a well-designed city park.

The colonists brought with them a piece of home. A place to come and think, to dream, and to recharge after a day of living on a spaceship. The only missing component were the people. Humans were all the park needed to make it complete. Almost at the same time, they stepped over to the closest bench and sat down to marvel at their discovery.

Chris informed Al the park had a blurb in the brochure. "I read it was here, but I had no idea it would be this nice. You see, the ship is designed using modules, and the modules are reconfigured to make up the different sections. The park and the farm are parts of one module and originally designed for the first ship. Over the years, they improved and refined the tech until they created this state-of-the-art module. There are fruit trees here: peach, apple, orange, and even pear trees."

Al asked, "All this for three months? Weren't they supposed to go down to the planet after they arrived?"

"They were, but they would have to live onboard until they were able to get down to the planet and get set up. The ship would remain in orbit to assist the colonists for years afterward with medical facilities, seed storage, and building materials. All the supplies could remain aboard the ship until needed."

"How about shuttles?" inquired Al.

"I think the brochure said five shuttles, capable of twenty-five passengers each."

"So somewhere on this ship is our ticket out of here?"

Chris grimaced, "Yeah, if we knew how to fly one, and we're not a billion miles from nowhere."

They talked for a while longer and then got up to wander the park. Strolling down the moonlit path, they passed the fruit trees Chris mentioned and helped themselves to an apple. At the end of the footpath, they entered the airlock for the next module labeled MEDICAL BAY and HIBERNATION UNIT STORAGE.

"Now we're getting somewhere," remarked Al.

The secondary hatch opened onto a long hallway, both sides of which made up an extensive medical bay. The lights were on only in the hall and the rooms on both sides were left dark and foreboding. There were foggy plastic panels on both sides of the hall that helped little in allowing them to see into the medical offices.

Doors were located on both sides, each with lettering stating their use. They stepped through a door marked *Recovery,* and the lighting quickly increased to expose the interior. Six hospital beds were arranged around the room, with medical equipment surrounding each of them; waiting for their first patients.

"I wish I could have woke up here," Al confided to Chris. "When I woke up, I thought I was having a nightmare."

"Me too," Chris replied. "My mom is here somewhere; I hope she can wake up in one of these beds."

"You mother is here?"

"She's the one that helped me get aboard. They claimed the lottery was totally unbiased, but it does help to know the right people," Chris proudly informed Al, "She is the senior electrical engineer on this ship."

Al put his hand on Chris's shoulder, smiled and said, "Lucky you. Not everyone has a mother like that. I think the hibernation units are in the next room, let's see if we can find her."

The Hibernation Unit Storage (also known as Hiber-Pod Bay) was dark and quiet. Tiny lights outlined the walkways, with the rest of the room cloaked in shadow. Standing on end, tilted just a little, and resembling tombstones, was a room full of hiber-pods. Row after row of blinking lights, indicating the status of each pod, reminded Al of colored fireflies on a summer night.

They stepped up to the closest pod to get a better look. Instead of a name, there was only the number four. A small glowing window allowed them to see the face of a man, maybe thirty years old, with brown hair, and the slightest of smiles. A foggy mist of coolant flowed around his peaceful sleeping face.

The pod indicator lights were blinking green, which was a good indication he was still alive. There was some in this sleeping crowd that were not so lucky. An occasional blinking red light meant some of these people were not okay, and might never see the end of their trip.

They moved to a pod with the blinking red lights. Determining if it was a man or a woman was difficult. Whoever it was, they died a long time ago.

"We need to find my mother before it's too late." Chris was worried and with good reason.

Al had come to a realization. "There are no names and a lot of pods. We need to know the number assigned each person to find your mother. With the fog in the windows, it might be hard to recognize her. Maybe, if we can find a working computer terminal, we can look it up, or it's possible there is a handwritten list stored somewhere for emergencies. Let's look around and see what we can find."

Small offices lined the outer walls of the hiber-pod bay, and they systematically searched them. The lights came on when they entered these rooms, and the search progressed quickly.

In one office Al found a safe with a card reader and a key slot. He tried his card, but nothing happened, so he continued his search. All the computer terminals were off-line or without power; it was impossible to tell which. Working towards the end of the module, they searched all the offices and checked all the cabinets and drawers that were not locked. They found nothing useful and met at the door at the far end of the bay.

That is when Al remembered the keys he found in Al Clark's room.

"I've got keys!" he exclaimed. Al reached into his pocket, grabbed the keys, and held them up for Chris to see with a big smile on his face.

"Yeah...so?"

"Follow me," Al said. He turned around and headed back to the office that held the safe.

Chris fell a little behind as Al rushed back, so he entered the room to find Al trying one of the keys and sliding his card. He kept trying different keys until on his third attempt the safe popped open.

"I found these keys in the cabinet with my gun and my card." Al pulled the door open.

"I've never seen keys like that," Chris said.

"That might be because they are from way before your time. It makes sense they would use these old keys to add a second layer of security to the access of highly secure areas. They are almost impossible to find and hard to reproduce. If these are Al Clark's keys, he had a high-security clearance."

In the contents of the small safe was a single thin journal. On the cover, in faded lettering, were the words: Hibernation Unit Code List. The journal was old and dry, and they had to handle it with care. Still, the little book was precisely what they needed.

****

THE JOURNAL WAS A BACK-up for a back-up. A code book that referenced names to numbers and was the last line of defense in case the records were lost. It was abbreviated and crude, but it told them what they needed to know. On the left side was a line of numbers starting with one and increasing on down the page. To the right of the numbers was a row of names with the top name being Tobias Effinger. Following the line to the right side of the page led to a description; Captain, Commanding Officer, EC-Excaliber.

Chris's mother was number twenty-six. Her name was Elizabeth Morris, and she was in pod number twenty-six with her position listed as Chief Electrical Engineer.

Chris was delighted, and wanted to go wake her right away. However, Al cautioned, "I don't think it's that simple. Do you know how to operate a hiber-pod?"

"How hard can it be?" Chris asked.

Al was not so certain. In spite of his doubts he said, "All right, let's go and see."

They returned to the hiber-pod bay, and it didn't take long for Chris to locate his mother's pod. She was one of the lucky ones. The indicator lights on the outside of the pod were all flashing green. Elizabeth was a very attractive woman, and Al thought her face looked serene and beautiful. The fog in the pod obscured the details, but he could tell she had the same blonde hair as her son—only longer. The resemblance to Chris was startling.

Under the flashing lights on the control panel, was a small cover that popped open when pushed on, and inside were gauges, buttons, dials and more lights. One troubling tiny light glowed a steady crimson. Operation of the pod appeared complicated, and there was no button or knob labeled WAKE UP. If the process was done improperly, it could kill the person inside. They looked at each other and said almost simultaneously, "We need a manual."

They left Chris's mother to her dreams and headed back to their quarters. Along the way, they each grabbed another piece of fruit from the trees in the park; Al tried an orange, and Chris another apple. They ate them without speaking, each thinking thoughts of their own.

In their quarters, Chris ate a package from the mess hall. Al decided he wasn't hungry. They each opened a bottle of water and sat down at the table to plan their next move.

Chris was disappointed. "Surely they have manuals somewhere for the hiber-pods. I can't believe we didn't find any."

His hopes had gone sky high when they found the journal. When they realized they didn't know how to operate the units, his hopes fell.

"I take it you and your mother are close?" asked Al.

Chris sighed and answered, "Yeah, she's great. She and my dad are both great. I was fortunate to have them for parents."

The look on his face turned sad as he told Al of his mother and father, and the decisions they had to make regarding the trip to Avalon.

Chris was the only child of Elizabeth and Thomas Morris. Both successful professionals with the income that accompanies it. He had gone to the best of schools and graduated as valedictorian of his senior class in high school. He graduated third in his class at college. Afterwards, he started an apprenticeship in advanced ship propulsion and was ready to start his second year when he got the call for the trip to Avalon.

His mother and father surprised him with a party the night before they left. A party they would never forget; a bittersweet celebration that would be the last occasion they celebrated together. Chris's father was happy for his wife and son. Unfortunately, he did not make the lottery and had to be left behind.

His father talked to him that night, "Sometimes things don't go the way you would prefer. I can't go—but you and your mother must. I will be happy in the knowledge that the two of you will have a better life."

They called Chris to the ship the next day, the day before it left. He arrived early in the morning, ushered aboard, and taken directly to the room where his hibernation pod was. The man that helped him into the pod said this spot was supposed to be filled by an experienced propulsion engineer, and that he was one, of only two, with hiber units located outside the hiber-pod bay. He was very fortunate.

In their rush to get underway, he had missed orientation, and the walk-through that the other passengers received; despite the late notice, he had made it. He was going to Avalon, and his mother was going with him.

"My mom will know a lot more about the ship...when we wake her." Chris told Al between yawns. "Where do you think we should look first for a manual?"

Al's answer was thoughtful, "It just makes sense to me they would store the manuals somewhere in the medical or hiber-pod bays. We probably need to try the keys I have, and see if there are cabinets or drawers that we missed that can be unlocked."

They had a plan, so with renewed hope they retired to their separate rooms to try and get some sleep. Visions of what might be made them restless, and kept them from a good night's sleep.

Chapter Five

There were no clocks visible anywhere. Al assumed the computer terminals were the means for telling time when they were functional. Time would be what they made it. To them, it felt like early morning when they awoke and headed to the medical bay to start their search. There was no time for a shower or breakfast.

Al only had four keys, so it didn't take long for them to try the keys in the locked storage spaces. They searched all the offices, all the cabinets, and all the drawers of the medical bay. Where the keys worked, they found medical books, hypodermic injectors, some complicated looking meters, and other sensitive medical equipment. The rest required keys they did not have, so they moved on to the hiber-pod bay and began searching there.

After what seemed like hours, they found what they sought. In a back office was a tall cabinet where the last key Al tried allowed them to open the doors. *Isn't it always the last one?* Inside was a stack of thick Hibernation Unit Operation Manuals. These too were old and fragile and required careful treatment. However, inside the manuals were the procedures they needed to wake Chris's mother.

Chris picked one up and grew increasingly discouraged as he flipped through the pages. "This may take a little longer than I thought."

Al heard the disappointment in his voice and offered, "We can do this Chris—but it's not going to come easy."

"Why would they build a machine that is so complicated?" Chris asked.

"These machines have to maintain a person, in all aspects, for many years on very little power. It's a miracle they could build them at all."

"Yeah, I guess you're right," Chris admitted.

Chris said he was hungry, so they each grabbed a manual and made their way to the mess hall to get some lunch and digest the information contained in the books.

****

THE MANUALS WERE VERY extensive and detailed. After they finished eating a quick lunch, they went back to their quarters to dig in and continue processing the information contained in the manuals.

Chris said, "I miss my comp pad a lot. If I had my pad, we could listen to music. Music helps me when I study." He smiled and added, "We could probably even get a step-by-step procedure on how to wake someone from a hibernation pod off the net."

Although Al had no memory of his past, he knew of the portable electronic devices used for so many things. "When we wake your mother, I think she might be able to restore the computers. I'm sure they have a music database of some kind on a colony ship, and I wouldn't be surprised at all if they had some personal data pads stashed around here somewhere."

"That would be great," admitted Chris, "For now, I'll just have to learn without music."

While reading through the different sections of the manual, Al was struck with a feeling of déjà vu. He had heard or read this material before. Sometime in his life, he had been familiar with this book or one very much like it. The more he read, the stronger the feeling became, and in time, he became sure he knew how to revive someone from hibernation. What he didn't know, was the meaning of the steady red light on Elizabeth's inner control panel.

The books they found were basic operational manuals, written so that any ship member could follow the procedures when all indicator lights were green. The manual stressed the all-green conditions, and emergency procedures had not been included. There was nothing about what to do if something went wrong. The subject could encounter falling blood pressure, increased heart rate, brain damage, breathing problems, and so on. Any of these could cripple or kill the occupant. There was no information on the tiny red light in the manuals they had, and it concerned Al.

"I think we might need a technician," suggested Al. "Your mom's pod has that red light, and I don't know what it means. Did you find any mention of it?"

"No, and I've looked everywhere," Chris admitted.

"Let's look in the code book," Al suggested. "Let's see if we can find a hiber-pod technician that has all green lights on the pod controls. I think I can wake the technician if the lights are all green, and then the technician can wake your mother."

Chris liked Al's idea and immediately stood to get the code book. He was gone only a minute and came back with a pen, a fresh pad of paper, and the precious book.

He held up the pen and pad and with a wink said, "Old tech."

Al laughed and shook his head, "I do remember those."

Before long, Chris had a list of twelve names with the higher ranks arranged at the top.

"This is all there is. I only added the ones that said they were hibernation specialists."

Chris handed the list to Al, who took a quick look and said, "This will do nicely. Are you ready to go back?"

"I can't wait."

They did not run, but it wasn't far from it. When the two castaways arrived at the airlock leading to the spoke lift, and were opening the hatch, Al heard a distant whine coming their way—and getting louder fast. He asked, "Do you hear that?"

Chris looked at Al with surprise and listened. "Hear what?" Oh,...that? What is that?"

The approaching whine became a scream, and grew increasingly louder with the corridor amplifying the sound; propelling it down the passageway until....

"It's a robot—look out!" Chris cried.

It was indeed a robot. A small, three-foot tall mechanoid, rolling on a single ball and coming full blast towards them. It seemed intent on going as fast as possible in a forward direction—in their direction. Right down the middle of the corridor. Both impending victims wasted no time moving from the center of the passageway.

Al realized that if the robot hit the door, as fast as it was going, it could damage the door and possibly make it unusable. They might lose the use of the one reliable lift to the rest of the ship.

"Quick, jump over here Chris!" Al yelled. Chris leaped to join Al, and just as the robot went past them, Al braced his back against the wall and kicked. The little mechanical assassin ricocheted off the wall next to the door, leaving a deep dent, and then the wall across from them to go struggling back the way it came. They could hear the screech of motors as it attempted to return to its suicidal run. Luckily, it only traveled ten feet or so before it started wobbling like a drunken sailor, made a few slow, erratic circles, and fell to the floor.

Chris stood there stunned. When he could finally speak, he asked, "What was that all about?"

"I have no idea."

"How did you do that?"

Al was dismissive. "What...Oh, I don't know. It just kind of happened. I was afraid it might damage the door."

"Holy mackerel! I have never seen reflexes so fast. You sure put the hurt to it. I might have to start calling you, 'Al, the robot killer.' Ha—you are the robot killer that killed a killer robot."

Al didn't find it quite as funny as Chris apparently did.

They walked over to take a closer look at this crazy little machine. After a short inspection, they agreed the broken robot was likely to be one of the ship's service units.

"It was probably designed to clean and maintain the ring," suggested Al.

Maybe half as wide as it was tall, it was cylindrical and moved about on a basketball sized sphere with a rough surface that protruded from the bottom. Three spindly, extendable arms, equipped with various tools and pincers, lay crumpled against its body. Its pale blue paint was scratched up and splotchy. On its torso was a faded red number nine.

The poor thing was not 'dead.' It was, however, banged up pretty good. Al became aware of a muffled whisper coming from a speaker simulating a mouth, and knelt down to hear...*Sorry*, being repeated over and over. He asked Chris to bend down and listen, so he could join Al in wondering why this robot would attack them, and then be sorry for it.

They left the broken robot, picked up the manual and their list they dropped during the rampage, and rode the lift up to the hub. From there, they made their way to the hiber-pod bay.

The robot episode they left behind, to be replaced by the problem at hand. How to wake someone safely from a long hibernation.

After a thorough search, there was only one hiber-pod technician with all green lights from the list of twelve. Only one lacked the troubling red light under the door to the control panel. The lucky person's name was Anastasia Kossalowski.

"She's young," Al said to Chris.

"And she's cute," Chris said with a grin.

"Yeah, but can she help us?"

"The list says she is a hiber-pod technician. She's the only one with all green lights and our only real chance. We have to wake her up," Chris pointed out.

Al reluctantly agreed.

The standard restoration procedure was not all that difficult if you knew a few things. Once activated, most of the revival process is automatically performed by the pod. A person just had to know which buttons to press, when to push those buttons, and how to set the timer.

They worked together, Al pushed the buttons and Chris double-checked him with the manual. When it came to setting the timer, they discussed it and decided to use the recommended six hour time table for maximum safety. If they adjusted the timer for less, it naturally raised the risk of something going wrong. They weren't in that big a hurry.

When Al pressed the last switch, a digital timer appeared, and steadily began counting down from six hours. The glow brightened inside the pod, making the girl's face look all the more angelic as the light flooded her features, and reflected off the backs of the pods before her. Deep inside the unit, a soft, steady, ticking began.

They decided to leave her for an hour. The risk was very low in the beginning, so they ran back to their quarters, cleaned up, grabbed a little something to eat and drink, and ran back. When they passed the place where the robot attacked them, they noticed the strange mechanical creature was missing, with no sign of it having been there—except the dent beside the door. Chris grabbed a blanket and a bottle of water for the girl in the pod, and Al grabbed some clothes for her, water for them, and some food packs. They went back to get comfortable and wait for her to wake up from her long slumber.

While they waited, they talked. Chris was nervous and did most of the talking, while Al mostly listened.

"How old do you think she is?"

"About your age?"

"Yeah, she looks about eighteen—maybe nineteen. Does she look old enough to be a technician? What if she can't wake my mother?"

"We'll have to wait and see."

"You will like my mom—everybody does. She's a great engineer that loves her work. My dad cried when we left. It was the first time I'd ever seen that." Chris hesitated, his face sad, and added, "I'm gonna miss him. Should we check the pod again?"

"If you want, I just checked it, though."

"Any idea why that crazy robot acted like that? It could have killed us."

"It was crazy—wasn't it," Al admitted.

Chris continued to rattle on, "Where do you think we are?"

Al chuckled, "We could be anywhere. We know we're in a ship, that's a beginning."

The humor went right over his head, and Chris continued, "I haven't seen an observation area yet, have you? Maybe there's one past the bridge door. If I had designed this ship, I would put the windows in front of the ring, so you'd have an unobstructed view of what's in front of you. Do you think your keys will help open the bridge door?"

"I didn't see a place for a key, but I didn't look all that closely," Al replied while thinking, *this is going to be a long five hours.*

Thirty minutes before the timer reached zero, there was the sound of a whining motor, and the front of the pod slid down into the floor. The mist inside disappeared, and they got their first good look at Anastasia.

She was dressed in a tight-fitting silver suit and was so short and petite she reminded Al of a china doll—a fragile doll at that. Her hair was short and brown, parted in the middle, and her appearance made her look as if she fell asleep only hours ago.

The timer reduced itself to thirty seconds, and she groaned. Her eyes popped open, and she looked around wildly for a moment before asking, "Where the hell am I?"

The timer clicked to zero, and an alarm sounded.

****

SHE TRIED TO TAKE A step out of the hiber-pod and began to fall. Chris was there to catch her and laid her down on the blanket they spread out on the floor. After a few minutes, the confused young woman recovered enough for them to talk.

"This is not at all what they told me. I was supposed to wake up on a soft fluffy bed, with friendly people all around me in white coats and name tags that said, *Hibernation Specialist.* Where are your name tags? Where are the white coats?"

Al was quick to explain, "Anastasia, we don't have any white coats or name tags for that matter. For some reason, we are the only people awake on this ship. Something has gone terribly wrong, and we woke you because we need your help."

She shook her head, paused for a second, and said, "Nobody calls me Anastasia. That name is way too formal and takes too long to say. Everybody calls me Ana. What is it you need *me* to do?"

Al and Chris took turns filling her in on what they knew. She asked an occasional question, but for the most part, she just listened. Al told her of his experience when he woke up and his subsequent amnesia. Chris followed with his awakening, and the year he spent alone exploring the ring. They told her how they met, their discoveries since then, and explained their trepidations about waking his mother. They concluded with their run-in with the kamikaze robot and then what it took to wake her.

Ana grinned and said, "I want my money back. This is not what I signed up for." Al and Chris laughed, and it felt good. The new group of three was going to get along just fine.

Chris asked the question uppermost on his mind, "Just how old are you?"

Ana hesitated, and it looked like she might not answer, until she did. Something about the question made her indignant. "I just turned twenty-one before we left. Why? Does that matter?"

"No...no, it doesn't matter, I was just curious. You sure don't look that old," stuttered Chris.

She responded, "I'm a lot older than I look. It's been a problem most of my life."

Ana went on to explain she was a child prodigy. She graduated high school at fourteen, college at sixteen, and was now a certified hiber-pod technician. Because of all she had accomplished, she was always touchy about her age. They learned Ana was a china doll with brains and an attitude.

Still unsteady after her revival, they helped her over to Chris' mother's pod, where she inspected the control panel and gave them the meaning of the worrisome light.

"It's an indicator light warning us she has been asleep more than the recommended lifespan of the unit. It's a good thing you didn't try to wake her the standard way, there are specific treatments needed, and she might not have made it."

Ana needed food and rest, so they decided to take her to the habitat ring. One more day would make little difference to Chris's mother, and they wanted Ana at her best when she started the awakening procedure. One on each side, they helped her to the living quarters of the wheel.

On the way back, they scrounged clothes that were closer to her size, and when they strolled through the park, they picked some fruit from the overburdened trees to take back with them. Her favorite was the apples.

Chris and Al set her up in the quarters next to theirs, where she could have some privacy and still be close. The two men returned to their quarters and left her alone to get a shower, eat, and rest.

Three hours later, she was outside their quarters and knocking on their door.

"I'm tired of sleeping. I think I've had enough sleep to last the rest of my life...so isn't there something we should be doing?"

They invited her into the room and offered her a seat at the little table. Ana said she had showered, changed into her clean coveralls, laid on the bed for two hours, and decided she couldn't sit still any longer.

She informed them, "We need to get some things together before we can revive your mother. She's going to have to be moved to the medical center before she wakes up, so we're going to need a floating stretcher. Most of the stuff we'll need will be in the medical center. We'll also need to prepare the recovery room.

Al nodded and said, "I'm ready if you are. How about you, Chris?"

"I have been dreaming about this for a very long time. You better believe I am ready."

"Let's grab what we might need and take it with us," suggested Al, "It may be a while before we get back."

They didn't have a lot to pack, so it wasn't long before they were on their way to the hiber-pod bay. Ana liked *flying* almost as much as Chris, and she was pretty good. However, they had little time to play and moved on.

The lights came on as soon as they entered the recovery room in the medical center.

Chris looked around and told Ana, "We've been all over this place. There is not much here."

She smiled and tapped her foot on the floor, "Most of the good stuff is under here."

Ana's revelation proved correct. There were small recessed handles in the floor that opened panels, and underneath was the real inventory of the medical center. The storage space below was more than adequate, with room for everything a modern medical facility needed.

"They did that because it was the safest place to store things for the long journey. Once we got to Avalon, we could unpack it all and be ready for patients in about a day."

Chris admitted, "Actually, it's kind of smart storing everything underneath. I sure never thought of it."

"There are all kinds of things under these floors. Space inside a starship is not wasted, and there is a lot of space. When you walk into any of these modules, you only see about two-thirds of what's there—you didn't get the tour?"

Chris glanced at Al, grimaced, and replied, "No, we missed that. It sounds like it might have been fun."

"And very helpful," Al added.

"Yeah, that too."

Chapter Six

They were ready to wake Elizabeth, with everything laid out on tables by a bed in the recovery room. Everything Ana might need was within arm's reach. This attempt would be the first time she had to perform this procedure. No person on Earth had slept this long, and, therefore, there was no precedent for waking someone after the recommended length of service of a hibernation pod. She would have to count on her skill and training to pull this off.

She programmed the pod for this unusual type of revival and set the timer for eight hours.

"You mother has been asleep for a long time, and she is not young. It's going to take a little longer to do this safely," she warned her anxious companions.

They stepped back and got comfortable; settling in for the long wait. The two men were asleep within an hour, but Ana stayed awake and monitored the hiber-pod. She wasn't able to sleep anyway.

When the front of the pod slid down, thirty minutes before the timer went off, Ana told the suddenly awake men to put Elizabeth on the floating stretcher. They floated her to the medical center, where they transferred her to the bed they had prepared.

Elizabeth looked drawn and gray as she lay before them. Ana hooked her up to the machines that would monitor her vitals and quickly administered two injections. The bed was equipped with an internal I.V. unit, which she hooked up and then opened the valves to allow the fluids she had prepared to enter her veins.

"Now we wait," Ana said, peering at Chris.

"I've got all my fingers crossed—that's not bad luck...is it?" he asked while grinning.

Ana replied, "Don't be ridiculous."

Al laughed, and Chris tried to act embarrassed.

Elizabeth's color slowly improved. She started breathing more regularly and soon after, her eyes began to blink. After an hour in recovery, her eyes finally opened.

She looked around, noticed Chris, and with a voice he could barely hear she whispered, "Christopher, what are you doing here?"

"I'm here to welcome my mother to the waking world," Chris declared. "Aren't you glad to see me?"

"Um...of course I am Christopher. You kept showing up in my dreams. Now, what is happening? You're not the people who were to wake me. Is everything ok?"

Ana admonished, "You need to rest for a little while before you talk too much."

While she was waking up, they slowly told her their stories, and without ceremony or fanfare, she became the fourth member of their party—a small group of two young people, and two not so young.

Al asked if she recognized him, and her thoughtful reply was, "I'm sorry...Mister Clark, but I don't recall ever meeting you."

She preferred to be called Liz, and like Ana hesitated to tell her age, except for an entirely different reason. She finally admitted to being a little over forty.

She was tall for a woman at five-ten and thin, with long blonde hair and blue eyes that reflected her confidence and drive. Al guessed she was not going to be laying around for long. They stayed with her for several hours and then used the floating gurney to move her to the habitat ring. Ana relocated into a larger quarters across the hall, and Liz moved in with her. As expected, Liz was quick to recover. Within a few hours, she was up and helping Ana make their place more livable.

Ana wished out loud, "It sure would be nice to have some sheets and pillows, and maybe some towels."

"Why don't you ask the service bots? They'll get whatever we need."

"I don't know how to call them with the computer terminals down."

"We don't need a terminal. There are three hab bots per section in this habitat ring. They're stored under the floor of the corridor when they aren't needed—here; I'll show you."

Liz got up and walked out to the passageway, with Ana following right behind. On the floor in the middle of the corridor was a faint circle, with a button on the wall and a tiny *Service* label. Liz pushed the button, and a small open lift rose up from below. They boarded the elevator and pressed the down button.

Under the floor was a small room with three robots lined up; waiting for orders. Liz stepped in front of the first robot, which had several small dents on its pale blue body, and said, "Robot Nine, we require sheets, light blankets, pillows, and towels for four people." She smiled at Ana and added, "Also, find some colonists work clothes for Anastasia Kossalowski and Elizabeth Morris, and...coffee, with cream and sugar. Bring everything to Living Quarters number fourteen."

Robot Nine acknowledged the order, boarded the lift, and within thirty seconds he disappeared with the lift. When the platform came back down, Ana and Liz returned to their quarters and resumed setting up their apartment.

Fifteen minutes later the robot returned with their bedding and towels. It was leaving their quarters and headed down the corridor for its second trip when Chris and Al opened their door and stepped out.

Al saw it first and yelled, "Hey...robot."

The robot stopped, turned around and said, "How may I be of service?"

"Come closer," Al ordered.

The robot beeped and then advanced to stop in front of them.

Al asked Chris, "Didn't the robot that went nuts have a nine on it?"

"Yes, it did."

"Why did you try to kill us?" Al challenged the robot.

"I am sorry sir. I did not try to kill you—I was experiencing a malfunction."

Al thought, *That must have been some experience.* "Are you done malfunctioning?"

"Yes sir, I was taken to the robotics shop and repaired."

"And you won't be banging into walls anymore?"

"Not if I can help it, sir. The walls are very strong."

It appeared to be functioning correctly. Although, there was an unusual touch of humor. Al chuckled and said, "Ok...well...carry-on."

The two women overheard the commotion and joined the men in the hallway. The four humans watched as the little robot rolled away to return to its duties.

"Nice robot," Ana said.

"Yeah, if you like killer robots," answered Chris. "That one almost ran us over." He grinned and turned to Al, "What if he's not telling the truth about being repaired?"

Al just smiled. Everybody knows that robots can't lie.

****

THEY GATHERED IN THE women's quarters to eat and discuss their next move. Four people in a massive sleeping ship facing some serious decisions. Still, they were alive and awake, and they had options.

"What do we do now, Mom? Wake the captain?" Chris asked.

Liz replied, "The original plan was to wake a hiber-pod technician, who would then wake a doctor, and then the two would wake another technician. When there were two technicians and a doctor available, they could revive the captain."

Liz was a member of senior staff and knew the ship well. She was on board for almost a year before they left Earth's orbit, and had become very familiar with the spacecraft. Inside a secret compartment in her pod, a storage space only her hand could open, was her top clearance key card. Al was glad they revived her. Things would go much more smoothly now.

She continued, "I would like to try and restore the computer terminals. The computer could tell us a lot. The passenger access was shut down for the trip, and if everything is undamaged, it shouldn't take much to get them back online. If we had working terminals, we could get the list of *who* to wake up *when* and a lot more."

Chris volunteered, "I could go with you. Maybe Al could help Ana get ready for more patients?"

Al suggested, "We could also make a list of the doctors and check to see what condition they are in."

They decided Al and Ana would prepare to revive more people. Chris and his mother would go to restore the terminals. They spent a couple of hours talking and getting to know each other and then returned to their separate quarters with their blankets, sheets, and pillows to get some rest.

In the morning, there was coffee and breakfast packages, and then they gathered their things and went their separate ways to begin bringing their ship back to life.

Chapter Seven

Chris and his mother headed for the computer relay station located in the center of the ring. As they rode the lift up to the hub, she explained what they needed to do.

"There is a relay in the hub that is fed from the ship's computer located beneath the shuttle bay. We need to close a few breakers and re-establish the link to the passenger terminals. Pretty simple really."

Chris unexpectedly admitted, "I am so glad you're here Mom."

Liz looked at her son, a worried look on her face, "You've had a rough time here. How are you—I mean really?"

"I'm okay Mom. Things are much better now. If you want to know how I managed my time alone, you'll have to read my journal. I even did some drawings."

She smiled at him and touched his cheek. "I look forward to that." She took a step back and looked him up and down, "You've grown so much, and you act just like your father."

He replied, "I should be so lucky."

"You miss him, don't you?"

"Yes, mom, very much."

"I miss him too," she said, and added, "They say time heals all wounds."

"I hope that's true Mom, I really do."

Suddenly uncomfortable, she changed the subject, "You need a haircut. I'm gonna have to take care of that."

Chris grinned, shook his head and opened the lift hatch. In the hub, the lights came on, and he made a quick three-sixty around the circular room; gracefully returning to his mother.

"I couldn't help myself," he said.

"I understand that, but we've got work to do."

"Yes, Mother."

The panel they needed was embedded in the wall by the main ship door. Liz opened the panel, reset the breakers, and realigned the signal. A small screen in the compartment lit up with the *Excalibur* logo, and just that quickly their task was complete. The terminals were online.

They couldn't help themselves from spending a few minutes playing in the hub before they headed back.

****

AL RETRIEVED THE CODEBOOK, and he and Ana sat down to work on their list. Going through the ledger was a tedious and time-consuming job. Rank was used to arrange the book instead of by profession, which required them to go through the entire list looking for doctors. They found four doctors and one surgeon before Al heard the room's computer powering up.

"Computers are up," he told Ana.

"All right!" She exclaimed, "Now we can find out what we need the easy way."

She jumped up and ran to the desk to find the *Excalibur* logo displayed on the monitor with a flashing telltale that stated—*Ready for input.*

"Computer, show me a list arranged by priority, of the people to wake when we reach Avalon. Display the first twelve names."

It took only a few moments to find the doctor they needed.

"It looks like we need to find a Doctor Ian Trask, pod number one-hundred and four. He was to be the third person revived," Ana explained to Al.

Ana's mind jumped to a new question. "Computer, what is our current location?"

"You location is the habitat ring—LQ fourteen," said the computer in a strong woman's voice.

"Not us—you idiot—the ship."

"Insufficient information."

"What do you mean, insufficient information?"

"Sensors are currently off-line," the computer answered.

"Why?"

"Cause unknown."

They were blind without sensors, as the computer had no way to determine where they were.

"Computer, what is the current date?"

"The current date is December twenty-first, two thousand two hundred and one."

Ana frowned and looked at Al, "We left Earth *more* than forty years ago? Did we miss Avalon?"

Al found the information disheartening, and admitted, "We could be just outside our solar system or ten years past Avalon, we just won't know until we get the sensors back. Let's get ready to wake the doctor, and then we can wake our other technician, and then the captain. When we get to that point, maybe we can worry more about where in space we are."

"One problem at a time—right?" she asked.

"Exactly."

They met up with Chris and Liz on their way to the lift and together they went to the hiber-pod bay to find a doctor. To their dismay, Doctor Ian Traskow died years ago. He was a shrunken, dried-out facsimile of a human being, and would never help anyone again.

Second on their list, was Doctor Jacody Mumbada. When they located his pod, they found a pleasant looking black man around thirty years old that was a trauma care doctor and a cardiac specialist. According to the computer, he was Doctor Traskow's backup replacement. His pod also had the troubling red light, but he was reasonably young, and through the mist in the window he appeared healthy.

Ana prepared the hiber-pod to begin the revival cycle, and set the timer for eight hours, as she had done with Liz. She stayed behind to monitor Doctor Mumbada's pod while the rest of them prepared the medical center. After they completed their preparations, the four of them sat down to discuss the second hiber-pod technician they required.

The name that the computer suggested was not the technician that Ana wanted to wake. She had a friend aboard.

"I know this woman—I've worked with her before I came to the ship, and she is an excellent technician."

"Shouldn't we be following the computer recommendations," reminded Liz. She believed in *by the book* procedures.

Ana was quick to reply, "I need to know I have someone I can work with. Under these conditions, we don't have time for personality clashes."

"I think Ana is right," Al said, "We do have to get along with one another if we're going to speed this up."

Eventually, Liz reconsidered, and they decided to wake Ana's friend. Chris was for whatever Ana was for, so Elizabeth was effectively outvoted.

When the doctor's pod slid open, Chris and Al loaded him onto the floating stretcher and took him to the medical center. Once there and under Ana's care, he recovered quickly, his first words were—of course, "Where Am I?"

His new shipmates went through the explanation process again, introducing themselves and informing the physician of their plight. Ana continued to administer to Doctor Mumbada while the others went to prepare for another awakening. They only needed one more person, and they could wake the captain. Hopefully, when he joined them, the highly trained and experienced officer could start making sense of their situation.

Al was elected to return to the habitat ring and have the robots prepare a room for the doctor. Liz told him how to access the robot's storage space, and tired of sitting, he grabbed his stuff and got moving. An hour later, he was in the robots cubby hole and standing in front of robot number nine.

"Robot Nine, I need you and your two friends to prepare quarters just aft of mine for Doctor Jacody Mumbada. He will require bedding, towels, and work clothing. Because he's a doctor, he will need a portable medical kit. Can you do all that?"

"Yes, sir. I can procure what you request. Will he require coffee?"

Al smiled and said, "Sure, why not?"

"Is that all, sir?"

"Yes...but give me a minute to get out of your way before you leave. I don't want you or your friends to run me over."

The robot beeped, hesitated for a second, and then in a little higher voice; it said, "I would never do that sir. We are programmed not to cause damage; to anyone or anything. What good is a robot that hurts people and breaks things?"

"Well—keep that in mind."

"Yes, sir."

Al boarded the lift and rode it up to the corridor. As soon as he stepped off, the platform went back down to pick up the habitat robots. When the little elevator returned, the three little robots scurried down the corridor to fulfill Al's orders. He figured he had some time to query the computer about Al Clark, and this was the perfect time to do it.

"No data available," the computer replied.

"How about..., the habitat ring, orange section, quarters number twenty-five? The room labeled Al Clark."

"No data available."

Al was perplexed. *"Did Al Clark even exist?"*

He asked the computer to search for any information concerning Al Clark. He tried Alvin Clark, Albert Clark, Al*Clark.

"No data available."

He was not going to learn anything. The computer had no record of him. Disappointed, he got up and left to see if he could help the others. He could hear them coming down the spoke long before he saw them, the sound of the lift echoing with people's voices and laughter.

The ship was slowly coming alive, and the chatter of happy people improved Al's mood. He was waiting in the airlock when the lift doors slid open, and laughter exploded into the airlock.

"The doctor believes in voodoo," Chris proclaimed. "Doctor Mumbada is from Haiti."

With a refined Haitian accent, the doctor was trying to explain, "That is not what I said. What I did say is medicine comes in many forms."

Chris shot back, "I'm just saying if I find a little doll made of straw under my pillow, I'm coming to see you first."

The doctor was laughing and shaking his head. "You are a silly boy, Christopher."

After they had installed him in his quarters, they gave him a couple of hours to pull himself together, and then gathered once again in the women's quarters. Robot Nine procured an extra chair, and they made room for the doctor at the table.

He was a tall, light featured black man with short black hair, deep brown eyes, and spoke his English with a slight accent. He was the kind of person where all you had to do was see him, hear a few sentences, and you could make a good guess where he came from.

Al asked him, "What's all this about voodoo, Doctor Mumbada?"

"Please, call me Cody. I much prefer that. We are all one family now, and we do not need to be so formal. I was just explaining to young Chris, that our world is a mysterious place, and there are many things we do not understand. One must keep an open mind."

"So, you're saying that voodoo is real?" Ana asked.

"Having spent most of my childhood in Haiti, I have seen many amazing things. Voodoo is not always meant to be evil, and the power to influence another person's mind can be useful for many things."

Young Chris had a fresh hair cut, and looking younger still; he chided, "I'm still gonna be checking under my pillow."

The conversation made Al feel hopeful. These were the kind of people that could save their piece of humanity, and it looked like they might have a little fun along the way.

****

THE NAME OF ANA'S FRIEND was Kayla Hamilton, and they found her in the same troubling condition as the others; excepting Ana and poor Dr. Traskow. The little red light was prevalent through most of the hiber-pod bay, and why Ana's pod did not would remain a mystery.

They revived Ana's friend with no problems, told her of their plight, and settled her into quarters of her own. Before long she had cleaned up, eaten, and was ready to go to work.

Kayla was a sweet, thoughtful woman. One of those rare people who listened more than she spoke. She paid attention to whatever you said, and made every person she spoke with feel special. She was in her early thirties, with dark brown hair cut short, mesmerizing green eyes, and had no trouble finding a place in the group.

She was elated to see Ana was the technician that woke her.

Now they had everyone they needed.
It was time to wake the captain.

Chapter Eight

Captain Tobias Effinger was a career officer and an excellent pilot. He only signed up for the mission because once the *Excalibur* established a stable orbit, he would be free to fly the versatile little shuttles back and forth to Avalon. Liz met him several times at different functions and got the impression of a friendly, no-nonsense type of person. He confided in her that his application was almost turned down due to his age.

He was fifty-two and past his prime. However, he still turned out to be the best candidate for the job—at least the best they had left on Earth.

When they gathered around the captain's pod, they discovered an additional problem. His pod had red lights on the outside, and under the cover of the control panel, there were more crimson warnings. The meter monitoring his heartbeat registered twice the normal rhythm and indicated the captain was quietly struggling for his life.

Ana, Kayla, and Doctor Cody huddled together to discuss this new development.

"We need to get him out of there as fast as possible," said the doctor. I'm afraid his heart is failing."

The two hiber-pod technicians looked doubtful.

"Have you ever revived someone in this condition?" Ana asked Kayla.

"Of course not. Most of my revivals were healthy people. I don't remember anything like this during training."

"Okay, we need to check the computer for hiber-pod emergency procedures. Maybe there is something in there that can help," Ana proclaimed.

The two women ran to the medical center to use one of the computer terminals, leaving the doctor to stare at a struggling patient he could not reach.

"Computer, show me emergency procedures for a hiber-pod occupant having heart problems," Ana requested.

The short delay of the response was aggravating, but after a few seconds, it displayed what they needed.

"Just as I thought, there is an accelerated two-hour cycle. We have got to go."

They rushed back and started the cycle. Two hours is a lifetime when it's life or death. They followed the procedure outlined by the computer, and when the pod finally opened up, the doctor took over.

"Okay quick, get him onto the stretcher and to the medical center."

Chris and Al did as the physician asked, and rushed him to a bed where the doctor could properly treat him. Ana and Kayla helped get the captain off the stretcher and onto the bed, hooked up to an I.V., and then prepare the machines the doctor requested. He asked Ana if she would like to assist, and told everyone else to leave.

The rest of the group waited outside and discussed the new developments. There were chairs in a small waiting room across the hall and through the two walls of thick dusty plastic, they could see fuzzy images of the doctor and Ana working feverishly to save the captain.

"Just in case, should we go and check the first officer's pod?" asked Chris.

"He's next in line so that would be the proper thing to do," offered Elizabeth.

Kayla asked, "If the captain doesn't make it. What if we can't wake the first officer?"

"What if we're not able to wake enough people to run the ship?" Chris wondered out aloud.

Elizabeth frowned in thought, and Al saw worry growing on the faces of his new-found friends.

"What if none of it matters, and we're a zillion miles from nowhere," added Chris.

Al interrupted their many questions, "I think we might be getting ahead of ourselves, we should have faith in both Ana and Doctor Cody."

He was trying to be the voice of reason, and could not allow panic to take over their thinking. "I think we should wait, and give them a chance to do what they do. Whatever happens, we can figure it out from there."

The surgery took a long time; seemingly forever. Eventually, bloody and tired, Ana came out to talk to them and to report that the doctor believed the captain had a good chance. "He will have to take it easy for a few days. In time, he should fully recover."

They moved Captain Effinger to one of the recovery rooms, and Cody accompanied them. The doctor requested a sleeping bag and had Robot Nine bring them their meals, who

Al temporarily assigned to the doctor. The robot seemed happy to be of service.

With Cody nearby, Ana and Kayla prepared to revive more people with the assistance of two service bots.

****

AL, CHRIS, AND LIZ went to see what they could do about restoring the sensors. All their future plans hinged on knowing where in the universe they were. Liz informed them the ship's sensor array was located below the shuttle bay in the main computer room. She led them through the hiber-pod bay and stopped by the airlock door leading to the next module. A faded sign spelled out, 'Shuttle Bay.'

Al was relieved that—to this point—there was little evidence of damage to the ship, excluding the large ragged hole in the green section of the ring. The Farm and Park module was well developed and appeared to have been operating for years with the help of the robots. As far as he could tell, the ship was remarkably intact.

Yes, the starship was old, but it seemed fundamentally sound.

The Hangar Bay was different.

When they opened the door into the hangar area, they found chaos. Pieces of debris littered the deck, and two of the five shuttles were damaged. One ship was beyond repair with a jagged twelve-inch hole driven through the middle. The ceiling of the hangar bay showed evidence of a similar sized hole and several smaller ones that had self-repaired.

On a long trip such as the one undertaken by the *Excalibur*, situations like this were anticipated, and the securing of everything that could become a projectile taken very seriously. It could have been a lot worse. Flying tools and parts can cause a considerable amount of damage. The parts liberated from the destroyed shuttle had crashed into the craft next to it, leaving numerous repairs necessary.

The path of the meteoroids was evident, and the flying rocks had continued through to the lower compartments. A rapid decompression occurred, and until the ship repaired itself, this area and the compartments below were open to space. In one of the compartments below was the computer room and the sensor arrays they sought.

"We need to get down there and check the computer," declared Liz.

They ran to the lift and rode it down to the computer room. While the seemingly slow elevator descended, more and more of the small room became visible until the culprit that caused the bulk of the damage was revealed. Lying in the center of the floor was the remains of a broken and scarred meteoroid, its energy spent. Before the lift stopped, Liz jumped off and ran to the main computer. She checked each component and was relieved to find little damage. A few sections had tiny holes bored into them which she inspected carefully.

"I need to run some tests, and probably replace a few circuit boards, but I think we're okay."

She turned around to peer at the sensor array, and said, "This, however, is a different story. It's going to take some work to get it back."

Numerous holes peppered the array components, and some pieces were missing entirely. They were going to be blind for a while longer.

****

THE CAPTAIN WAS AWAKE when they returned to the medical center, although still weak and pale. The people responsible for waking him gathered around his bed in the recovery room and made their introductions. To Liz, their new leader said, "Good to see you again." And then he said the same thing to Al.

"Do you know me?" It struck Al that he was talking to the captain, and he quickly added, "Sir."

The captain looked confused, and his eyebrows dipped. "You're my Security Chief...right?"

"I'm a Security Officer?"

The captain's confusion changed to concern, "Are you joking with me Mister Clark?"

"I'm sorry sir, but...have we met before?"

His eyes darted around the room, and the captain replied slowly, "Well...yes, just before departure. Are you all right?"

"I'm all right sir; I'm just having a little trouble with my memory."

"That is unfortunate." The captain hesitated, and then added, "I'm sure it will come back to you."

He appeared a little uncomfortable and quickly moved on to bigger concerns. He addressed all of them and asked for a status on their situation. They filled him in on what they knew, including the condition of the ship, the shuttles, and with the sensors down, that they were unable to determine their location.

"Elizabeth, I need you to take Mister Clark and get the sensors back online. The rest of you will concentrate on waking the rest of the crew according to the procedure outlined in the computer. We need to bring this ship back to operational status as quickly as possible and get on with the mission."

Captain Effinger asked the physician, "When can I get out of here and get to work?"

"Hold on sir. You just had heart surgery and are going to require a minimum of a few days in bed, and then a week or two of restricted duty. There is no sense in my saving you if you just turn around and kill yourself..., Sir."

"All right then, but let's try and hurry this up. From what you've told me, we have a lot of work to do. Oh...let's see what we can do about overriding the spoke lifts that are still usable. We're going to need as much access as we can get."

Their leader was awake, and now they had direction. The captain's new crew breathed a hopeful sigh of relief.

Chapter Nine

Al was feeling good. He now had a name and profession. The computer outlined his position and its requirements. However, it made no mention of who was to be in charge. Al assumed that he, like Chris, was a last-minute addition to the crew that someone had forgotten to add to the computer.

While Liz was busy doing repairs on the sensor array, he used a nearby terminal to find five security officers that met his criteria. He would discuss this with the captain, but Al thought a security team should be high on their list of priorities. It was not hard to find five men that were all experienced with exemplary records. Yes, he was feeling pretty good.

It made sense that he was security. The captain's statement explained many things: the uniform, the sidearm, the keys, and his high-security clearance. He thought that he was going to like this job, and was anxious to return to the orange section and set up his office.

Chris did what he could to assist the two hiber-pod technicians. It was not his field of study, but he was a good listener and followed orders willingly. They had awakened two more people; the first officer, and a helmsman. Both were now settling into their quarters.

The captain was recovering at a remarkable pace and was to be released to return to duty the following day.

It was Christmas Eve, and earlier in the day, the captain decided that a party was in order. He offered the use of the observation lounge, which was spacious enough for the number of people attending. After all, there were only ten of them. The group considered Robot Nine as one of them, and he was invited to play bartender and all around go-getter.

They gathered in the hub and practiced *flying* in the zero gravity until the captain arrived on a floating gurney with Doctor Cody driving. The makeshift crew was officially off-duty for the first time since their revival, and they were in the mood for a celebration.

Captain Effinger's condition was much improved, and he radiated confidence for the future. "Maybe we'll see something we recognize through large panoramic windows."

It was the captain's card that opened the door, and they entered one by one into the observation area. The sight of their lives awaited them. Silence ruled the moment as they were overwhelmed with what they saw out the large transparent window. The captain's wish had come true, and they finally knew where they were.

Slowly circling below them was the most beautiful planet they had ever seen. Clear blue skies with a sprinkling of cloud cover hovered over the landscape. Land complete with mountains topped in white, green valleys, and massive rolling flatlands.

The oceans were immense and blue, reflecting the sunlight back to their eyes. There was not a hint of pollution, flat tracks of land, or even cities. What they looked down on could only be Avalon.

When the realization sunk in; pandemonium broke out. Everyone was talking at once, and except for the captain, was jumping up and down and yelling. Cody had to hold their leader down to keep him from following their example.

They took turns looking at the planet through the small telescope mounted in the lounge, and they toasted each other. They talked about their future and drank some more.

They toasted Christmas Day as it rolled around, and marveled at the fantastic present slowly spinning below them. Robot Nine served drinks while they danced and drank until the entire planet turned and displayed itself before their hungry eyes.

It was the best party any of them had ever been to, or would ever attend. All that was necessary now was to get down there, and a little later than planned—they would finally be home.

****

THERE WAS ALWAYS A price to pay for a party such as the one they had. Al was the lucky one because, after the first couple sips, he decided he probably didn't drink. The party lasted until morning, and almost everyone else had a hangover to contend with the next day.

They continued bringing the ship alive, though, and soon the corridors were echoing with the sound of people, equipment, and habitat robots. With more humans now awake and settling in, the robots were in high demand.

Robot Nine seemed attached to Al and was always nearby. He tried sending it away to assist other people, but it always came back; awaiting his orders.

The original six individuals to wake first were assigned quarters close to each other and stayed good friends. Known as the *First Six*, most of the colonists considered them the saviors of Excalibur, and of the people inside.

With all the additional people to help, repairs on the computer and sensor array were completed, and repairs of the remaining shuttles were well under way. The captain scheduled planetfall for the following month, and with the help of the sensors, they accumulated data on the planet and picked the most likely landing sites.

"Computer, how long have we been at Avalon?" Al queried.

"Stable orbit was established ten years, two months and twelve days ago."

Ten years wasted! It still shocked Al.

"Why was no one revived when we arrived?"

"The revival circuits were disabled."

"Do you mean disabled...or damaged?" pressed Al.

"Disabled."

"By a human?"

"Affirmative."

"Do you know who disabled the revival circuits?"

"No data available."

Someone or someones, back on Earth, had wanted this sleeping ship to circle their new home until it was inhabited only by the dead. Their final destination was only miles away, and yet—unattainable.

Why would anyone want that? Al wondered.

Later that day, the first six gathered at Liz and Chris's quarters to talk about their day and unwind. Even though they were tired, they wanted the latest news before retiring.

"The ship was sabotaged?" Ana asked Al.

"It sure looks that way. I asked the computer in as many ways as I could think of and always wound up with the same conclusion."

The possibility of sabotage was hard to imagine. That someone would want to doom over a thousand innocent people to a long, slow death, was beyond comprehension.

"There must be some mistake. I do not think it possible," Cody proclaimed.

Al squirmed in his seat, "I find it hard to believe too. Still, there it is."

Kayla spoke up, "I remember a group of people that were convinced the colony ship program was a waste of time, resources, and money. The group claimed the colony ships were for the conquest of other planets. They believed the lottery was rigged and only the wealthy and elite would be allowed aboard. They were a pretty powerful group and called themselves *'Earth First,'* I think. They were always in the news feeds....Do you think they could have done this?"

After a while, the group decided it didn't matter. They were here, and they were awake. The universe had intervened and made things right. After forty years, the settlers were now preparing to leave the ship and make a home on Avalon.

Al was in the shuttle bay settling a minor dispute when the captain came to inspect the now pristine and organized area. Over the affections of a woman, one of the subjects had become so angry he took a swing at the other who promptly reported it to security. Al didn't mind, if this were the worst he had to deal with, he could live with it.

The captain strolled onto the shuttle bay followed by a small entourage and went straight to the head mechanic. "How are the repairs coming on the shuttles?"

"We will be ready by planetfall, sir," The man replied with confidence.

"Have you performed any test flights?"

"No sir, we didn't feel it necessary just yet."

The captain, not usually prone to anger, had to restrain himself as he said, "I want every shuttle thoroughly tested before the first passenger is allowed to board. You only have three weeks before we will need them. Do you understand these spacecraft have been sitting around for years and will require exercise and testing?"

"Yes sir, I will get right on that," the red-faced mechanic answered.

"Have you been presented with a pilot roster yet?"

"Umm—not quite yet sir."

"Well get it done, and make sure you add me to the list."

"But Captain, you can't....

"The hell I can't. Nobody tells me I can't fly. You are dismissed."

The captain noticed Al standing to the side, winked, and turned around to leave with his group. Al was impressed. The captain knew what he wanted, and just how to get it done. Not all commanders were as capable.

****

THE SURVIVING MEMBERS of the crew and the scientific complement were all revived, and the hiber-pod technicians were busy awakening the colonists. Ana and Kayla were very busy and pushed themselves to stick to their schedule. This period would be their most active while they were awakening people. Once they revived the last colonist, their duties would change considerably.

Chris was helping to repair the shuttles. He was good at his job and loved working on the tough, versatile, flying machines. Whenever he got together with any of the group, he found it hard to talk about anything else.

His mother was also busy, as was Cody. All of them were gearing up for planetfall.

Al, however, was bored. With everyone aboard preoccupied, nobody had time to cause trouble. He spent his days walking around under the guise of patrolling. He was in constant communication with his five security officers. However, they too were bored. There was not a lot of chatter over the radios.

He would stop and visit his friends from time to time. Because they didn't have a lot of time to chat, he would move on. Sometimes, he would stop at the mess hall, talking to anyone who stopped long enough to listen. He walked the park several times a day; simply because he could.

There were a few cases of a robot misinterpreting someone's orders, sometimes with some pretty hilarious consequences, and a couple of fist fights. Most of the time, Al walked around and became acquainted with the people he was tasked to protect.

In their off hours, Chris and Al took to playing racquetball in the hub. Originally it was meant to be exercise, but it turned out to be a lot of fun also. The game was much harder without gravity and led to a lot of unintended reactions.

A strong net was installed behind them to act as support. Even with the netting, it was tricky to keep the ball in play. They laughed until it hurt. People came to watch and laughed with them. Some even worked up the nerve to try their luck, and by the time they were ready to begin planetfall, crowds were betting on who would win. In the beginning, Chris was usually favored to win their matches. Toward the end, the odds swung to support Al. The bored security chief thought his travels while patrolling the ship helped his game.

****

ORBITAL OBSERVATION revealed a planet brimming with plant and animal life. Sun drenched valleys rolled gently up to snow-capped mountains, and swift streams meandered down towards the deep blue oceans. It was the Earth of days gone by with forests and prairies covering half of the landmass on the planet, with smaller islands to rival the old Jamaica or Hawaii of Earth. In a word, Avalon was paradise.

Several remote landing sites were selected and then narrowed down until they settled on one primary site. On the largest landmass, relatively close to the equator, they found their new home. It sat at the foot of a rust-colored mountain, in a green valley close to a lazy blue river, and it was the perfect place to establish the first colony of Avalon—a place they named Shangri-La.

They would be landing in early spring, and the homesteaders would have the best part of spring plus all of summer and fall to prepare for winter. Average temperatures on the surface would be near ideal until then.

An exploratory flight to the surface was scheduled and the crew members selected. Aboard the shuttle would be: Al and two of his security people, a biologist to document and collect samples of the local flora and fauna, Doctor Cody in case of injury or illness, a habitat coordinator, a co-pilot, and the captain—acting as the pilot because they couldn't talk him out of it.

The *Excalibur* was operating smoothly, and the captain/pilot had a good excuse to fly, so he left his quite capable first officer to manage the ship in his absence.

The captain recognized the possibility of encountering indigenous natives and therefore decided to make landfall just before sunrise, coming straight down from the sky quickly to minimize exposure. They would stay two days.

The lucky crew members selected for the first trip were instant celebrities. They would be the first humans to set foot on Avalon, with Al the most recognized mainly because he knew so many people from walking the ship. Everywhere he went people congratulated him and grilled him with questions.

"What do you think it will be like?"

"Are there large animals?"

"Will the natives accept us? How advanced are they?"

"Can we eat the plants down there?"

"Is the water safe to drink?"

Al would smile at each question and reply, "We won't know until we get there."

****

THE NIGHT BEFORE PLANETFALL a bon voyage party was held in Chris and Liz's quarters. Al, Chris, Ana, Liz, Doc Cody, and Kayla had all found time to be there. Al's first six friends in his new life, and the closest thing he had to a family. They relaxed and snacked on fruit from the park, discussing whatever came to mind.

"Why do you think the captain wants to go so bad? Shouldn't he be staying aboard the *Excalibur*?" Elizabeth asked the group.

Chris and Ana were sitting on the bed, and Chris responded to his mother's question, "If I were the captain, I would sure want to go."

"He is most likely curious as to what we will be dealing with down there," Cody suggested. "And I have heard that he enjoys flying the shuttlecrafts."

"Maybe he just wants to get away from the responsibilities of command for a while," said Ana.

Al respected their leader and liked his command style. He had to say something in his defense. "Why shouldn't he go? Our captain is responsible for everyone on this ship. He wants to be the first to assess the safety of his people on the planet, and besides, he has a full staff of competent officers to take care of the *Excalibur* in his absence. Personally, I welcome his company. How much can happen in only two days?"

Chapter Ten

The hangar bay was full, with standing room only at departure. Ship security set up barricades for a wide aisle down the middle of the shuttle bay to contain the crowd. The first humans to visit Avalon filed in and boarded among cheers and whistles, with the captain boarding last.

When Al stepped up to the aircraft, he turned to the crowd and waved, hamming it up while thinking of the age-old tradition of cheering and throwing confetti when a cruise ship leaves the dock. He was excited to be leaving, actually feeling sorry for the people that had to stay.

Al traded his formal off-white uniform for a more practical pair of khakis and a tan short sleeve shirt with his Chief stripes sewn on the sleeves. He even considered a pith helmet, like they wear in the tropics, but thought that would have been a little too much. Even without the helmet, the outfit made him feel like an explorer.

The planetary team seated themselves while the captain closed the doors and started the engines. The shuttle floated slowly up and maneuvered to the hangar bay door where a force field twinkled to life. The large outside door slowly opened and slid up out of the way to reveal black space and bright stars. Without hesitation, the shuttle smoothly accelerated through the opening, circled over the *Excalibur*, and pointed itself at Avalon.

The captain stopped the ship, set the controls to stationary, and turned to the passenger compartment, "Al, I believe you have some rules you'd like to lay out?"

Al addressed the group seated around him. "Everyone is aware of the rules—right? We go everywhere in twos, and we stay close to camp. If you need to go out of sight of the shuttle, a security officer will accompany you. We keep our voices down—if you need to yell, you use the radios, and we don't touch *anything* without gloves. Remember, this is only a preliminary survey. We will be carefully taking samples and returning them to the ship to be analyzed. There is no need to take unnecessary risks. Are there any questions?"

There were no questions. It was evident his crewmates wanted to get going. When the captain saw there was no reason to delay, he turned his attention back to the controls and said, "All right then—let's go and see our new home."

They descended to within a mile of the surface and directly over their designated site. The craft hovered for a moment, weightless and silent; and the passengers held their breath without knowing.

The captain said, "Here we go," and they dropped like a rock into the night sky.

The ride down was a blur of clouds and a rush of air that shook the shuttle. When the shuttle fell to within a hundred feet of the ground, the captain gradually added power until they came to a stop; floating inches off the ground. It was a ride to remember. The captain knew his shuttle and its capabilities. He smiled all the way down.

Al asked, "Is that why they call it planetfall?"

The captain just smiled. He parked the shuttle under a large, unusual looking tree at the edge of a forest of exotic timber, where the group constructed a fold-up canopy of camouflage netting twice as large as the craft. They used the extra space under the canopy as a covert base. Out of sight equals out of mind.

Before unloading, they gathered and watched the sunrise. Slowly, as the sun came up, their new world was revealed to them. The mountains were to their south, with a green and purple forest flowing up to them. To the north was a picturesque river, with spring thaws from the mountains adding to its girth. Green rolling hills with clumps of tiny red and blue flowers stretched all the way to the river bank. The name they picked was well chosen—it truly was an Avalonian Shangri-La.

They were not, however, fooled by its beauty. The planet appeared similar to Earth. However, all they had to do was look around, and it became obvious they were not on Earth. Evolution works differently according to different requirements and has varying results. Every plant and every creature they saw would be an entirely new species.

Tables were set-up and various scientific equipment placed on top. Afterwards, everyone helped to collect specimens and samples. They recorded the location of each item collected, along with any particulars, and then the specimens and samples were safely packed away into air-tight cases. It was the beginning of a long busy day, but nobody complained.

Taken in by the landscape, and with little to do, the captain and Al took a stroll down to the river around mid-morning.

The sky was clear, and the air was fresh. If not for the alien life all around them, it might have been a perfect spring morning at home.

Al was helping Cody to store the sample cases when the captain asked if he would like to take a walk. Earlier, Al noticed the captain surreptitiously watching him several times. When Al would turn in his direction, the ship's captain would look away.

While they walked, Al tried to find out why. "Is everything all right, Captain?"

"Sure...everything is fine. How about you?"

"I'm all right sir."

The captain stopped on the bank overlooking the river and took a deep breath; enjoying the view. Unexpectedly, he turned to Al and said, "I've been wanting to talk to you, Mister Clark. Are you doing all right? I mean with your amnesia and all."

The question surprised Al. "Well...I still can't remember anything that happened before I woke up in the pod, but I'm doing fine otherwise."

"It doesn't appear to affect your duties," the captain pointed out.

"Oh, no sir, I seem to remember a lot of things...just not about me.

"That must be terrible. Would you like to know more about yourself?"

"Very much sir. I don't let it eat at me. Although it does concern me."

The captain looked down at his feet and then raised his head to look Al in the eyes, "I'm hoping it will come back to you. Everyone should know their past."

Al nodded and replied, "It would sure be nice to know my real name, even if I can't remember the rest."

In the middle of the river, something surfaced, splashed, and slipped back underwater. Al and the captain stood on the bank, watching the river to see if it happened again. Later, Al would wonder if maybe the captain knew more than he was saying.

****

THE SUN BEGAN TO SET, and the explorers retreated to their shelter. They paused from their efforts long enough to watch the sun go down. It was a sunset to rival many of Earth's end of day spectacles, and it made more than a few of them homesick.

After dark, they held their lighting to a minimum with only enough light to finish their cataloging, run some basic tests and prepare for the next day's efforts. The team worked quickly knowing they had only one more day to gather all the information they could before they packed up and left; just after sunset the following day.

Earlier in the day, Doctor Cody and the biologist, Dr. Nestling, found some animal tracks in the mud by the river. There were tracks all over, but these stood out because they were eight inches long, with three long claws in the front and one in the back. They found only two prints in the mud—as if it had appeared, and then suddenly disappeared.

Some of the group were crowded around a terminal, puzzling over the 3D images Cody and the doctor recorded using a data pad. The monitor allowed them a larger view.

"Looks like a big chicken to me," one of Al's men suggested with a wink.

"This chicken stands five or six feet tall, and could very possibly be dangerous," the biologist retorted. "We should be careful."

The captain warned everyone to keep their eyes open and report anything unusual, or that might be dangerous. "Do not forget—this is not Earth."

The team ate when they could. Some managed to get a few hours' sleep. The sounds of the forest and the river permeated the air, and in the distance, they heard an occasional unearthly howl. As the night wore on, they became increasingly aware of how vulnerable they were.

Al and his men were up the whole night watching the camp perimeter—for big chickens—or anything else that might cause a threat. He and his men were armed with MLP handguns, and the shuttle held three laser rifles capable of taking out a bear at three-hundred yards. Al was not taking any chances.

In the morning, they were too busy to watch the sunrise. There were bugs to collect, soil samples to get, and 3D images to record. The camp was abuzz with activity as they attempted to accomplish all that was needed before they left. At daylight, most of the team left camp to go out and finish their work.

At the base of a tree nearby, a security officer and the town planner discovered a basket. It was a primitive, hand-woven container fashioned from reeds collected by the river, and it overflowed with colorful fruit. They found it early on their way to document habitat locations and immediately brought it back to camp. When they returned, the co-pilot was the only one left at camp. He asked, "Where did you find it?"

The security officer pointed. "Right there...Not a hundred feet from us. We had three security men on watch all night, and they still managed to get that close without being seen."

The co-pilot confirmed their fears. "Well...so much for our being discreet. It looks like somebody knows we're here."

They called the security chief and informed Al of the find. "You found a what? Where?"

"A basket sir...at the base of a tree about a hundred feet from camp. I don't know how they did it."

Al was helping to collect water samples from the riverbank, and this news was unsettling.

His officer said, "It's a basket full of fruit sir—a fruit basket—I think it's a gift,"

"You mean like welcome to the neighborhood?"

"I'm afraid so, sir."

The captain is not going to like this, thought Al. *The presence of natives nearby will complicate things.*

When the captain heard about the appearance of the basket, he was not pleased, although, he took it better than anticipated. It was inevitable that first contact would happen sooner, rather than later.

"We'll finish our mission as planned and leave as soon as it gets dark enough. Make sure that everyone is aware and ready."

The captain explained his thinking by saying, "This is our new home. Like it or not, we'll have to learn to live with whoever is here. We have nowhere else to go."

All the samples and specimens were safely packed away onto the shuttle, and everyone on board was talking about the basket and the many things they had learned on Avalon. Al was in the back seat watching the forest as the shuttle lifted off.

In the gloom, standing in the shadow of the woods, a silhouette of something taller than six feet was watching. It appeared their departure was being observed.

Chapter Eleven

The shuttle bay was full again as the first humans on Avalon returned. Everyone had a thousand questions, so the captain held up his hands and got the crowd to settle down long enough to say, "Initial findings of our primary site are promising, and it appears suitable to our needs. It is not quite as secluded as we had hoped. It seems the planet is inhabited, and we have neighbors.

"The mission...is a success, and we will post all our results on the shipboard net. Habitat modules will begin going down starting next week, followed shortly by personnel." With a broad smile, he added, "Welcome home everyone!"

The returning team left the shuttle bay the same way they came—with cheers and whistles. The attention was nice. However, what they wanted most was to get cleaned up, get something to eat, and to rest. All the way through the hiber-pod bay, the medical bay, the park, the farm, and on to the habitat ring, they answered questions. The group responded when they could but politely kept moving. They had begun a new branch of human history, and it left them excited and tired.

Al was not too tired for a welcome home party. The doctor declared he couldn't keep his eyes open, so he went home to get some sleep. Al and the rest of his friends gathered at Ana and Kayla's to celebrate their return. Of course, his friends also had questions.

"A fruit basket...really?" asked Ana.

"A nice one, with shiny, colorful fruit in a hand-made basket; of reeds no less."

"What do you think it means?" Liz wanted to know.

"Somebody wants to make friends?" offered Al.

Chris, looking thoughtful, said, "It sounds like the Avalonians are pretty primitive. Do you think it might be a tribute?"

"I don't want to speculate—let's call it a basket of fruit for now."

"Is the water drinkable?" inquired Kayla.

"Tests so far are good. We will have to wait until the rest of the analyses are completed to determine if treatment might be necessary to make it safe. I am told it looks good so far."

"What are the trees like?"

The discussions went on till late in the evening. Al answered their questions as best he could and told them what he knew of Avalon. They speculated on a dozen subjects, explained their personal theories, and laughed at each other's jokes. Al could have talked about Shangri-La and their trip all night. Eventually, someone said something about getting up in the morning and yawning, and the party reluctantly came to an end. Al left to get himself some well-deserved rest.

****

THE SECURITY CHIEF asked for and received permission to deploy two autonomous drones called *Watchers* at his earliest opportunity. Whoever it was that left the basket needed to be watched in return. As head of security, he was responsible for the safety of all the personnel sent down to establish their community, and he wanted to use all the tools available.

Al needed an early warning system and found just what he required underneath the floor in the security section. He knew what they were before he even opened the box. He opened one and removed the baseball sized drone that included technology rendering them effectively invisible. They could float in a tree or circle a specified area at five-hundred feet silent and unseen.

The Watchers were typically programmed to operate at a specified range from a center point. They could operate twenty-four-seven and had a three-hundred and sixty-degree field of view. If it detected unusual movement, heat or sound, it would move closer to investigate and transmit images to a security device along with an alarm.

He had to test them and surprised his officers more than once with his surveillance techniques in the days before departure. He would program the Watcher to target a particular individual, and it would follow discreetly behind them; oblivious to the fact they were being observed. When a disembodied voice from behind would tell them to pick the mashed potatoes over the green beans in the mess hall, Al found the expressions on their faces hilarious. They, however, disagreed.

The return to Avalon involved two shuttles. The captain decided he didn't want to risk more than two with only four shuttles left after the meteoroid strike through the shuttle bay.

Planetfall was as before, with the ships falling through the clouds before dawn to land by the forest. One ship would carry the first four habitat modules.

A habitat module consisted of a six by six cube that self-deployed into a twenty-four by twenty-four-foot self-contained habitat. The cubes could be stacked or added end to end to construct whatever dwelling was required. The modules were multi-purpose, versatile shelters that would serve as temporary quarters until more permanent buildings were built.

On board the second shuttle was: Al, two security officers, Elizabeth, the town planner, and a crew of specialists on habitat construction.

Upon arrival, Al left one security officer to patrol the grounds and took the other to help deploy the two Watchers. They programmed them to stay one-hundred and eighty degrees apart, and circle the perimeter of the construction site at an altitude of one-hundred feet. If a threat occurred, an alarm would be sent to all the officer's security pads.

Al issued specialized security devices to each officer the day they joined his team. The pads were small enough to fit in a pocket, and multi-purpose, with functions tailored for surveillance and communication.

The Watcher alarm includes live video, audio, and details such as distance, size, temperature, and speed. Al felt better once they were deployed. Now they would know if anything tried to sneak up on them.

They tested the response of each Watcher and then Al sent his officer back to help with the unloading. He decided to assist Elizabeth to install the satellite dish they would need to boost communication with the ship in orbit. She was busy unpacking when he arrived.

Al asked, knowing she was fluent in anything electronic, "Got any idea what you're doing?"

Her answer was quick, "Well...I think this thing gets connected to that thing, and then you add this little spiral thingy to the side of that thing, um...Add a few wires and bingo; you have instant communication with a spaceship in orbit."

"I don't think that's how it works."

Liz admitted, "It may be a little more complicated than that. I forgot to mention all the computer jargon."

Al chuckled and asked, "Need some help putting the things together? I can help with that."

"Sure—grab that box and follow me. We have to find an out-of-the-way clearing where we can do the install."

The satellite needed a direct line of sight to the ship, and an elevated position to protect it from animals and signal blockage. They found a spot just inside the camp perimeter, far from the people constructing the habitats. Before they could begin to unpack, Al received an alarm. Something triggered one of the surveillance drones, and the device in his pocket was screaming.

The intruders also heard the alarm and ducked for cover. Al took his pad from his pocket and opened it to see what the Watcher saw. A hundred feet away were two 'people,' hiding in the forest behind some bushes. The silent drone floated directly above them; invisible and unnoticed.

His radio squawked to life, "Come in Chief Clark. We just got an alarm, sir, and it appears you have company."

His officers in the camp saw the same information he did.

Al whispered to the device, "I have the alarm. Maintain your positions. I'll call if I need help."

He did not need a lot of people rushing to their rescue.

Elizabeth whispered, "What do we do?"

"I'm not sure. What's the protocol for first contact?"

"We are not ready for that."

Al grimaced, "I don't think we can wait until it's convenient."

"First contact has to be done very carefully, by trained people. In other words, anything you say can be taken wrong and sometimes with dangerous results—maybe we can sneak away?"

"I don't believe that's wise. I'm pretty sure they saw us—as well as heard us."

"All right Al, but we can't say anything more than we have to."

Together they stood up, walked to within twenty feet of the bushes where the others were hiding, and waited until the natives acknowledged them. Al could only take it for a minute or two before he finally said, "Hello...you can come out now."

They heard a short, subdued conversation in another language coming from the bushes, and two heads slowly poked above the greenery. Hesitantly, they stood up and came from behind the bushes, and immediately fell to their knees. Some fruit dropped from the baskets they were carrying which they hurriedly replaced. They were obviously scared.

Al held up his hands in what he hoped was a universal gesture of friendship, and they cowered even more. They were not just scared; they were terrified. Al knelt beside them and motioned for them to stand up. They grabbed the baskets and stood, holding the offerings out.

They were clearly humanoid and young. A little short by human standards, with the tallest one standing only about five-six, and the other a little shorter. They had long dark hair and dark eyes, were dressed in skins and furs, and carried pointed spears. The tall one had a belt over one shoulder fashioned from something resembling alligator skin.

It became apparent the taller one with the beard, was male, and the other female. If the two aliens were cleaned up, they could easily pass for humans.

Elizabeth and Al had a short discussion and decided it is only proper to trade a gift for a gift, so Al asked if she had anything to trade in her pack.

"I do have some chocolate."

Al couldn't help himself. "Does every woman carry spare chocolate with them?"

"Umm...sometimes?"

"I'm just kidding. Chocolate is perfect for this situation. Let's trade."

They each accepted a basket and Liz, in turn, handed each of the natives a bar of chocolate and pantomimed eating them. Their faces lit up, and they went back down on their knees. The two humans just shook their heads. This was not how they had imagined first contact would go.

Al thought it necessary they find out where the two lived. The natives watched spellbound as he knelt down and drew a rough plan of the valley in the dirt and explained his makeshift map.

"This is the forest. Over here is the river. Up there is the mountain." He pointed to them and then the map and asked, "Where do you come from?"

When the aliens figured out what Al was trying to ask, they pointed at a lower portion of the mountain while shaking their heads up and down. It seemed the gesture for yes *was* universal.

"That would explain how they knew we were in their valley, Liz. From where they live, regardless of our precautions—they saw us coming."

What do you say to two strangers from another world that can't understand a single word you say? You stand around smiling and nodding your head—a lot. Al knew there were experts on board *Excalibur* that would know just what to say. They were people trained for this kind of thing and spent most of their lives dreaming about it. Al also recognized that first contact, done incorrectly, could result in all sorts of accidental damage.

Al pointed at the natives, then the spot where they said they came from, and told them with a big smile, "Go home...you...go home." Liz followed his example, and eventually, the two young primitives started bowing and slowly walking backward. The humans smiled and nodded their heads until the natives were perhaps thirty feet away, at which point the first alien race ever seen by humankind turned and raced home.

Al and Liz watched them until they were out of sight, shook their heads a few times, and immediately returned to installing the satellite dish. They needed to call the ship as soon as possible. The captain needed to know about this impromptu meeting.

****

KIRA THE GIRL, AND Toji, the guy with the beard—ran. They were good at flight; having learned to run not long after they could walk. It was already late in the day, and they had to be *Home* before dark. However, there were daylight dangers in the woods, so they slowed a little as soon as the star gods were left far enough behind.

From the time they were little, they were taught to move swiftly and silently through the forest. On this occasion, the two young natives' excitement overrode their training, and they couldn't stop whispering. Their first meeting with the Kuthra had gone well, and they were coming back with gifts. The elders would be pleased.

Kira and Toji were specially picked to deliver the tribute due to their skills in the woods and were only expected to drop the baskets nearby and quietly slip away. The fact that they actually spoke to a Kuthra was beyond their wildest dreams.

The *Sansi* tribe watched the humans arrive and depart on their first visit in their remarkable flying machines. When the gods returned, the elders were convinced *The Prophecy* was coming true; where mighty gods came down from the star in the sky to help defeat the 'Riktors.' The prodigal saviors were coming to help them.

Kira and Toji scrambled up the path leading to their caves on light feet as the sun was setting, and so engrossed in their discussion that they almost ran into the crowd awaiting their return. The tribe hurried them into the main cave entrance and blocked it off with large, heavy boulders. They no longer left it open and posted guards, as posting guards outside—at night—usually ended badly.

The mountain was naturally riddled with caves, and this section was the indigenous people's homes. Over time, they systematically blocked all but a few entrances and made the mountain a safe place to live. In the past, hundreds lived here. Now, they were down to a few dozen.

They called themselves Sansi. Every person on Tiera—the native name for Avalon—were Sansi. Except for the Kuthra, of course, who came from the star in the sky.

There were no wars between Sansi for they were all too busy hiding from the Riktors. The beasts would suddenly appear and take their children, or kill the adults, and then take their children. They were the creatures that came in the night and a part of the natives' nightmares.

The Sansi elders watched the star that brought the gods for many cycles, and the elders had predicted that one day they would come to save the Sansi. The natives could not go outside to see the star at night, but it could be seen moving across the sky through small holes in the upper part of their cave. It was a special star, and many prayers had been addressed to it.

Kira and Toji's friends and relatives surrounded the two tribute deliverers, and when they were safe inside, they brought out the chocolate that the Kuthra had given them. They put their hands to their mouths and said in their tongue, "You eat it. It is food."

The senior before them accepted one of the chocolate bars and carefully opened the wrapper. He smelled it, broke off a tiny piece, and with a wince, put it into his mouth.

His face transformed into one of delight, and he proclaimed, "It is the food of the Gods!" The Sansi cheered.

Chapter Twelve

Establishment of the human camp progressed well the first day. By nightfall, they completed the construction of one habitat. There was no water in the shelter, and the solar cells had not had time to charge, but the simple building was ready for use.

The communication dish was operational, and Al and Liz were using it to inform the captain of their meeting with the two natives. He listened to their story and had a few direct questions.

"You gave them chocolate?"

Al admitted, "Umm...yes sir. I didn't think it would hurt, and they brought gifts for us."

The captain continued, "What else did you do?"

"There wasn't a whole lot we could do. We sent them home."

"Did they tell you where that is?"

"Yes sir, they pointed it out to us."

"Good. In the morning, send one of your Watchers to find them, and maybe get an idea as to how many there are."

"Will do Captain."

"You do realize you've probably ruined their diet and more than likely their teeth?"

"Sorry, sir."

"I'm going to send a contact specialist down on the next trip. She should arrive by tomorrow afternoon. Hey, while you're at it, send Liz back with the shuttle. We need her here to help wind the ship down."

"By your command...sir," Al said with a grin.

"What was that? The radio has some static."

"Never mind sir. Liz will be on the shuttle in the morning."

Al glanced at her to see both palms raised in a sign of submission.

"I'll talk to you again tomorrow. Good night sir." Al signed off thinking. *That could probably have gone better.* When he told Elizabeth what he was thinking, she laughed and agreed.

Later that evening they joined the rest of the colonists at a long table set up for dinner. The scientists, the habitat specialists, security, and pilots were all colonists now. One large family sitting down to dinner after dark. Lantern light helped set a relaxed mood and kindled conversation.

They were discussing the abundance of lizards. Avalon appeared to have a large population of all kinds of reptiles. There were some seen on the first trip, but now they seemed to be all over the woods. They were mostly small four-legged lizards, except one person reported one almost a foot long. Al listened to the discussion and began to get concerned. "Have you found any in camp?" he inquired.

"They seem to prefer the woods. I haven't seen any in the open," someone volunteered. Several others agreed.

"Has anyone been bitten?"

Everyone looked around. None spoke.

Al had a warning for them, "Well, you might want to avoid that. It is possible that some of them may be poisonous. Everyone should avoid them until we can learn more."

The Excalibur held powered sonic security fences designed to close off an area from mouse-sized animals to man-sized animals. To be on the safe side, Al decided that those fences would also be on the shuttle when it returned to camp tomorrow afternoon. Al told himself, *better safe than sorry*.

It was just about then an alarm went off. The security chief almost dropped his pad getting it out of his pocket. The device displayed a video of something big, moving fast in their direction. It came out of the west, with the Watcher right behind it. Al could see the creature's back moving side to side as it sped through the woods, rushing right towards them. The creature was at least eight feet tall, and fast; moving at thirty-seven miles per hour and not slowing down.

Al was unsnapping his weapon and preparing to yell orders when a second alarm pierced the night air. There was another one coming from the opposite direction, about the same size, and advancing at a similar ground eating speed.

He had two places he could send people to safety; the nearest shuttle parked sixty feet away or the habitat sitting ten feet closer. He told his two officers to head towards the last alarm and everybody else to head for the habitat. He hoped ten feet would make the difference.

The rifles were locked up in the farthest shuttle and too far away to help. It was a mistake Al would regret.

He ran from the canopy and headed west towards the habitat modules stored there. The cubes were placed out near the perimeter to get them out of the way until needed, so Al had to cover a lot of ground in a hurry. He wouldn't have guessed he could run that fast, but Al did, and he made it to the farthest cube quicker than he would have thought possible.

The monitor indicated it was close. He took a breath and looked around the side of the cube to see a ten-foot beast, in full predator mode, as it burst from the trees and ran straight at him.

It was a dinosaur. The history book kind with an enormous mouth, long pointed teeth, and strong hind legs that tore up the ground the creature left behind. A twelve-inch horn poked from its head, and it was thundering toward him.

He pointed his weapon and started firing. The MLP could recharge itself fast for many shots before a full recharge was needed because it was a small laser. It was not designed for distance and only made small holes. It wasn't helping.

The monster hit the cube head-on, impaling it on its horn, and driving it backward with Al sliding behind it. It then picked up the six-by-six, one thousand pound habitat, and threw it to the side; which left Al standing in the open and in shock. When it reared up and roared, Al ran for his life.

He made it to the shuttle with the rifles, thinking he might be able to get to the more powerful lasers. Unfortunately, there was no time. He turned and started firing at the creatures head. It was his only chance. If he didn't kill it, it was going to kill him, and he wasn't done living yet. After the fifth or sixth shot, it realized its mistake and tried to turn away, but it was too late for the already dying animal. The beast staggered, fell, and slid sideways to bounce off the shuttle; landing in a dusty heap next to Al.

Across the camp, someone was screaming. The monitor on his pad showed one of his men standing frozen in front of the second creature, and he realized the man was in serious trouble. Al raced to the opposite side of camp, past the other shuttle, past the canopy, and to the completed habitat; to try and help. He would be seconds too late.

The monster was already where the humans were hiding and ripping long jagged creases in the shelter with its horn and long talons. He could hear people screaming inside. One of his men was firing at it from a nearby construction machine, behind the creature, and the other man was lying by the beast in two bloody pieces. He needed to end this quickly.

Al joined the man firing and told him, "Get ready, and aim for the head!"

Al knew that the creature had to be facing them and close, for the pistols to be effective, so he jumped up and down and yelled, "Here we are. Come and get us."

The creature turned, roared, and turned to comply. It died before it realized what was happening and with a final scream fell hard at its victor's feet.

The conflict was over for now. Within a matter of minutes, they had killed two dinosaurs and lost one of their own. It was a hefty price indeed.

****

WHEN THE DUST SETTLED, the first thing that Al did was retrieve the rifles from the shuttle. He was going to keep them closer from now on and would not underestimate the inherent dangers of the planet again. This event would change their whole perspective of life on Avalon.

There were three rifles in the shuttle. Al and his remaining officer each took one, and the third he gave to one of the habitat specialists trained in its operation.

They crowded around a portable lantern placed on a small table inside the banged up habitat, and discussed what had happened. The body of the security officer was brought back to camp while the two dead beasts were left where they fell until morning. The attack convinced Al it was too dangerous to be out after dark.

Elizabeth was upset, as they all were. "That poor man didn't stand a chance." She added, "Why haven't we seen any sign of these things before now?"

"We did find those footprints by the river...although they were smaller." Suggested the town planner.

The security officer that survived the attack was still in shock. "It took out Rudy like he was a doll. We kept firing at it, and it just kept coming. Who would have thought we'd be attacked by dinosaurs, and that they would be so freaking fast."

Al agreed, "They did look like dinosaurs—didn't they?"

The town planner had been thinking and asked, "Did anyone notice the lizards? There must have been a dozen lizards running behind each of those creatures. Why would they do that?"

Al thought they were probably there for the left-overs, but he didn't verbalize it.

Liz gave Al a puzzled look and asked, "How did you make it all the way back from the other side of camp so fast? One minute I heard you firing out by the cubes and the next you were here saving us."

"I don't know...it all happened so fast...I didn't have time to think."

"You more than likely saved us all," she said, and then quickly realized her statement was not quite right.

"Not all of us," Al reminded her.

Al didn't feel like talking, especially about himself. He had lost one of those he was responsible for, and he would be obligated to speak at his wake. As his commanding officer, Al probably knew him better than most. Rudy was not just a fellow officer; he was a friend.

Al recommended the colonists pull back and regroup. They needed to rethink their whole settlement idea. If they were going to find a place on this planet and survive, they would have to change how things were done.

At daybreak, Al instructed one of the Watcher drones to perform a search for the area the natives indicated on his crude dirt map. The device found the natives on a ledge outside a network of caves on the side of the mountain. The Watcher rewarded him with a view of men going out hunting, kids playing, and elders sitting in the sun. Al decided to suggest the captain make arrangements for a meeting as soon as possible. The colonists needed to know what the natives knew.

Later that morning, they discovered the dinosaurs they killed were not as they left them. During the night they were devoured until all that was left was white bones. Everyone assumed the carnivorous lizards were responsible. The scientists wanted samples of the creatures to study, so a few bones were gathered and taken with them.

They followed the captain's orders to unload the shuttles and secure the site as best they could. Then everyone—including Rudy's body—returned to the Excalibur.

****

THEY HELD THE WAKE in the hangar bay, with Rudy's closed casket laying off to one side behind a podium. Al and his friends sat at a long table and watched while different people took turns speaking at the rostrum.

Rudy had no family aboard like most colonists. However, he did have a lot of close friends. He had been twenty-six and was not only a good security officer, he also held a master's degree in agriculture. Rudy was excited about Avalon and looked forward to transforming the planet into a garden world for the human race.

When it was Al's turn to speak, he was not ready. He still didn't know what he was going to say as he stepped up to the podium. The shocked crowd of almost three hundred people made Al more than a little nervous.

He started with, "Rudy Labronski will be missed."

Chief Clark stood looking at the crowd for a few seconds, listening to the murmur of agreement and clink of their glasses in a silent salute. The crowd seemed to agree.

"He was funny, smart, and easily likable."

As he spoke, the words came to him. "Rudy believed in this mission, and he couldn't wait to help this colony carve out a place on this planet. He told me more than once he was looking forward to the type of life we would be building. He had no family except us. We were his family. There were eight hundred and thirty-two people that survived the trip here, and as a contributing member, he played an important part. He gave his life to protect us."

Al wanted everyone to know the significance of Rudy's loss.

"Rudy was the first to die *on* Avalon, and he will be the first to die *for* Avalon. We have lost a friend, but his sacrifice was for a cause he believed in. Rudy would be glad no one else was hurt.

"For all we know, we could be the last people to leave Earth. If we were able to return to Earth, it would not be the Earth we ran from, only one much worse. This planet is where we settle the human race; right here on Avalon. Rudy knew that, and it excited him."

Al's mind took him back to a conversation they had in the shuttle on the way down to Avalon. Rudy had big plans for the colony; thinking ten and twenty years into the future.

"He was proud to be a member of this family, and I think he will be proud to be one of the first marked down in the Avalon history books. He will not only be remembered—Rudy Labroski will be famous.

Hesitant clapping accompanied Al to his seat. Most of them were unsure what was appropriate, with it being a wake and all. Still, they were all nodding approval.

The gray haired captain took the podium, cleared his throat, and said, "There is a personal file for every person aboard the *Excalibur*. In that file is a form that tells us what you want done with your remains in the event of your death. Rudy Labronski wanted to be buried on Avalon. It was his first and only choice. He added to the form, and included details such as: under a beautiful large tree, close to the mountains, with a river nearby. He was talking about Shangri-La."

Captain Effinger stopped, hesitated, and continued, "We have decided to honor his wish and bury him accordingly. His funeral will be the second thing done when we return to the planet. There will be two shuttles, with one for the funeral and room for twenty-five people and two pilots. The other shuttle we will load with equipment and personnel to secure the camp from predators. The funeral will not begin until the compound is declared safe."

He looked down and considered how to continue. "This is not the planet we hoped to find. It appears the long-ago dinosaurs of our Earth, didn't become extinct on Avalon. We will be sharing the land with these monsters and will have to make...adjustments.

"There will be security issues to deal with, and we will have to rely on each other to remain safe. Mister Clark is responsible for colony safety and needs to be informed of anything that appears remotely dangerous."

He gestured towards Al and nodded. Al grimaced a little and nodded back.

The captain finished with, "We will post departure times and the passenger lists when ready. Please, people, let's make Rudy proud."

The wake broke up around eight, and everyone went their separate ways. Life went on. The ones that knew him would remember him and move on. Those people that did not; would find moving on a little easier.

Al left to be alone with his thoughts, and he and Robot Nine took a walk in the park. The little robot was an excellent listener and only spoke when necessary. Strolling the cobblestone paths, with the trees and grass all around, helped him relax and think more clearly. He realized that colonizing this planet would be far harder than they could have imagined. The discovery of Earth's prehistoric equivalent of the dinosaurs would change how they settled Avalon considerably.

It became apparent that to live on this world; they would need the help of the people who have lived here for generations—The Avalonians.

Chapter Thirteen

When they returned to Shangri-La four days later, they found the site demolished. The canopy was in shreds, and the habitat cubes damaged beyond repair. The single standing habitat that saved their lives was now scattered and in ruins. Large reptilian footprints were everywhere, and it appeared the beasts destroyed the camp with great rage. It was decided this location was no place to create a home, and certainly no place to bury Rudy. It made no sense to cling to this spot that was beautiful, but impossible to defend. They didn't bother unpacking and received permission to return to the *Excalibur* to reconsider their choice of settlement sites.

After much discussion, it was decided to move the camp. A place was selected closer to the mountain, with their backs protected by stone cliffs and rough terrain. The natives were about a mile away, close enough to establish a relationship, and still far enough to keep the two settlements separated. The winding river was nearby for water, with a broad patch of open ground leading up to the camp.

This time, they went in force. Three shuttles were loaded with personnel and equipment and sent down to begin again at the new location. Their first priority was to construct a ten-foot sonic fence surrounding the construction site. They could enlarge the barrier later as they became more established and the settlement grew. The following day, the contact specialists would seek to arrange a meeting with the natives.

Additional security was recruited, and Al now had ten security officers under his command. He left four men on the ship and came down to the planet with six. Robot Nine was fitted with a laser and assigned to Al's department full time. Al found it ironic that the robot that had initially tried to kill him was now going to have his back.

They deployed the two Watchers to act as an early warning, and stationed them a quarter mile outside the fence perimeter, always circling above at one-hundred feet. The surveillance drones gave his security officers enough warning to save lives, and now more than ever he believed in them.

As soon as the fence was operational, they held the funeral for Rudy. It was not Shangri-La, but at least he would be close to his friends. They buried him under a tall tree overlooking the water, in the shadow of the magnificent mountain. Everyone agreed it was a beautiful spot.

His headstone read simply, *Rudy Labronski - To save some, he sacrificed all.*

The settlement was going to be permanent and would remain occupied at all times. The colonists held a contest for the name they would use, and after going through hundreds of entries, the winning name picked by the senior staff turned out to be—The Village of *Camelot*.

****

IT WAS TWO ALIEN CONTACT specialists, two armed security officers, Robot Nine, and Al that went to meet the natives. With four security personnel stationed on the ship, that left four to guard the camp. Al was confident that with the fence, and the aid of the Watchers, the colony would be safe in his absence. They kept the party small, so they wouldn't frighten the Avalonians and carried gifts with them: blankets, cooking pans, canteens, and chocolate, all of which they divided among the travelers to carry.

The party had their breakfast and left a half-hour after dawn. The specialists believed the predators did their hunting at night, so it should be safe to make the trek to the caves, have their meeting, and get back before dark. They did not take a shuttle, thinking it would scare the primitives into believing they were descending from wherever it is gods hang out. They wanted friends—not worshipers.

Robot Nine took point, with Al directly behind, followed by the specialists and then his men. The two contact experts, Cindy and Rahul, talked non-stop behind Al. They were heading towards the fulfillment of a lifetime ambition, and all they could do was argue. Cindy wanted a more structured approach while Rahul wanted the conversation to lead their discussion.

"We have to hear them out and give them a chance to take the lead. The more they talk to us, the more we learn from them," Rahul repeated for the third time.

"We should be asking the questions, and ask them what we need answers to," Cindy shot back. She was very set in her thinking and determined to be heard.

"How are they going to know what our questions are? They can't understand us." Rahul asked her.

The argument went back and forth for a long hour before Al finally turned to them and said, "Listen up you two. We are walking through unexplored territory, with unknown dangers, and predatory creatures that are drawn to noise. I believe when we get there, your training and education will take over and you will do just fine. Until then, let's concentrate on our surroundings and leave the disagreements until later."

Thirty minutes later, Robot Nine warned, "Movement up ahead."

Al saw it too, behind the occasional tree on each side shadows moved; never quite visible in the light. There were flashes of something almost seen.

Cindy noticed Al looking around and asked, "You see something, Mister Clark?"

"We are being watched...and followed," Al replied in a subdued voice.

A short time later Cindy asked her colleague, Rahul, "Do you see anything?"

"All I see are trees and a lot of grass."

The robot stopped for a second, turned to Al, and quietly reported, "They are staying well back sir, and appear to be just observing. It is possibly the indigenous humanoids. We are only a half-mile from their caves. Should we continue?"

One of his men from the back of the procession spoke up, "What's the holdup?"

"We think the natives are here, and keeping an eye on us," Al replied.

"So—they know we're coming?"

Al said, "If that's true it's a good thing. We don't want to surprise them. Is that right, Cindy?"

Cindy agreed, "It is better *not* to show up out of nowhere."

Al wanted to keep moving. Their time was limited before they needed to head back to camp. "We are almost there everybody, so keep your eyes open. Let's move on."

The natives were not surprised, and a welcoming party dressed in their finest furs and embellishments was waiting when they arrived. A dozen members of the tribe were lined up on their knees with their foreheads touching the ground; waiting for their gods to acknowledge them. The two young natives Al and Liz met were there kneeling with the others.

Al nodded at the specialists and Rahul took the lead. He walked across the line smiling and gesturing for them to stand. The natives hesitantly stood but kept their eyes firmly on the ground. Rahul positioned himself before the center individual, who appeared to be the eldest and the best dressed. He presented him with a bar of chocolate. The Elder accepted the gift with a broad smile and motioned for the youngest of his group to present the native's tribute.

The gift Rahul received was the most unique necklace Al had ever seen. It was woven from a fine colored hair that produced a thin sixteen-inch-long multi-colored chain of crafted beauty. The presenter removed it from around his neck and handed it to Rahul, who ceremoniously placed it around his neck.

"I call dibs on the necklace," he announced.

"You can't do that," Cindy protested.

"Okay you two," said Al.

When Rahul presented each of the welcoming party with a bar of chocolate, they were happy at first, until it occurred to some of them they had only one gift, and received twelve. Al could see their thoughts become conflicted. They were afraid the one necklace wasn't enough tribute. After the gods assured them their tribute was sufficient, they were invited up to the caves.

The uncertain natives ushered the visitors into a large room, with two dozen spectators standing respectfully to the side. Soft brushed hide pillows lay on flat rocks and acted as seats, and an abundance of food on a large wooden table waited for the visitor's pleasure.

The natives loosened up in time, and a stuttering dialog began. They all enjoyed the exotic food, and the delicious fare helped to put both groups at ease.

The specialists did most of the talking since they were the experts. There were universal gestures such as a nod meaning *yes* and a head shake meaning *no*. However, the bulk of communication was through facial expressions, pointing at various things, and drawing on the dirt floor.

The colonists learned a lot about their new home and its inhabitants that day. They were told the winters in the mountains were cold, and how much the natives loved the blankets given to them by their guests. With looks of amazement, they accepted the aluminum alloy cooking pots, and it became apparent the tribe would treasure the hard, shiny, cookery. The canteens, with their magical screw-top-caps and insulating coatings, would make carrying and storing water much easier; which the natives loved.

In time, the discussion turned to dangerous animals. There were many predators on Avalon, but the king of the meat eating beasts were the Riktors. The Sansi were terrified of the creatures that killed Rudy and almost always hunted in pairs.

They learned the two rampaging monsters killed by the settlers were part of a territorial group of ten or so, which terrorized and ate every native out after dark. The caves they were so proud of acted as their refuge, and provided shelter from the predators of Avalon for generations.

The natives were family oriented, intelligent, and loved to laugh. It took some time to explain the human's desire for one of the Sansi to visit the colonists at their camp. He or she would temporarily live with the settlers and learn the human language. The ability to communicate was the biggest stumbling block to their relationship, and the specialists deemed that teaching the natives English was priority one. In two days' time, one lucky Avalonian would be living with the Gods.

The natives escorted the colonists halfway to the settlement, and then rushed back to beat the coming darkness. The greeting party also hurried home.

****

THE RETURN TRIP WAS an easy walk, with three to four-foot greenery lining the path they followed, and they were making good time. Just outside the fence, and inside the Watchers perimeter, a bush reached out and grabbed Al's leg.

A long red tongue wrapped itself around his ankle and was trying to pull him to it. Al told everyone to get back, drew his sidearm, and put a hole into the attacking appendage. There was an anguished scream, and the tongue released him and retreated. A three foot tall cross between an anteater and an armadillo bolted out of the bush and disappeared into the woods. A few nearby bushes rattled as several others took the opportunity to do the same.

Al cried, "Whoa—what was that? It almost had me!" Ten feet in front of Al and at the front of the procession, was the robot. "Were you sleeping Robot Nine?"

The two arms facing him went up. "I am sorry, Al Clark. My sensors detected no dangers. I will add this new creature to my threat programs...and I do not sleep."

Al took a few steps and decided he could go on. He looked up at the darkening sky, and then to the people surrounding him.

"We better keep moving...it's getting late."

His leg didn't hurt much; it just felt a little tingly. It did not seem to affect his walking, and there were no cuts on his pant leg, so he figured it was all right. When they reached the fence, they collectively breathed a sigh of relief. Their first contact excursion was over.

As they passed through the gate, Al was struck by the progress they had already achieved. In only two days, the primitive camp was already changing into a little town. A soft hum permeated the air from portable power supplies, and lights were flickering on to keep the darkness at bay.

With all the added colonists, progress in Camelot was accelerating. The shuttles had unloaded and returned to the ship for more people and supplies. Four habitats were complete, with level surfaces prepared for four more. Most of the trees inside the perimeter had been cut down and used to make numerous forms of lumber. Nothing was left to waste with even the sawdust used to fill sidewalks to keep the mud down.

Al sent Robot Nine to make its rounds, checked with his men, and then sat down in one of the habitats to do some paperwork. He plugged in his data pad to recharge and bent down to raise his pant leg and check his ankle.

When he pulled the pant leg up, he was shocked by what he saw. An inch above his boot was a circular wound, with a red furrow that went through the skin and clear to the bone. He was horrified. He felt little pain, and there was not enough blood for it to be this bad.

How have I been walking around on this? Why doesn't it hurt like crazy?

He bent down further for a closer look.

The bone doesn't look white; it looks kind of...silver; and there are wires?

Al Clark grabbed a clean towel to wipe the blood away.

That is not bone; that's metal...I have a metal leg?

Al leaned back and took a deep breath. He was staring at the far wall with unseeing eyes; his mind busy with what this discovery might mean.

Are both legs artificial? Would that explain his ability to run? Don't both legs have to match to keep from falling?

A dozen possibilities scrolled through his mind, and with the world on hold, he sat unmoving for several minutes. One conclusion he came to was he needed help, and someone he could trust. He also knew Doc Cody was setting up one of the habitats as a clinic nearby, so he rolled his trouser leg down and went to see him.

The doctor was alone when he entered, and Al wasted no time showing him his leg.

"What on Earth....ah...what has happened to you?" Cody asked.

"I was attacked by a giant ant-eater/armadillo on the way back. The leg tingles, but it doesn't hurt, and I've been walking around on it for two hours since the attack. It hardly bothers me at all. Something else Doc...I think there is metal inside."

Doc smiled and asked Al, "Now why would you think that Mister Clark?"

"Take a look if you don't believe me."

After a quick examination, the doctor discovered Al was indeed correct.

"You did not know about this?" his friend asked.

"Umm—amnesia Doc, remember?"

"Oh...yes, sorry."

Doctor Cody was now intrigued. He told Al to sit on the bed, and Cody took a closer look. "I have never seen anything like this. Your leg does not look artificial. Please, lie down so I can scan it," ordered the doctor.

The portable scanner was already set up, and it took only a few minutes to complete the scan. Cody's face grew puzzled. He made some changes to the machine and scanned again, this time, the scanner went from head to toe. Al could see his face, but not the monitor he was looking at with wide eyes. Doc Cody's expression was puzzling.

"What do you see Cody?" Al begged.

The physician appeared deep in thought for a second; then he shook off whatever was clogging his thinking and locked the door. He pulled the curtains on the windows so no one could see inside. He returned to Al looking hesitant, flustered, and maybe a little scared.

"I do not know how to tell you this, my friend." He glanced again at the screen as if disbelieving his eyes. Cody turned to him with conflicted eyes and said, "It appears, Al...that you are not human."

Al jumped up and swung around to look at the monitor. What he saw was not what he expected to see inside a human body. The screen revealed mechanical and electrical components; with thin metal rods, micropumps, tiny circuit structures, and ribbons of complex wiring connecting everything together. Where his heart should be—a red power supply glowed.

"I'm a robot?"

Chapter Fourteen

Al almost laughed until he realized it might make him appear crazy. His reality had changed when Cody said those words. A flurry of thoughts became jumbled and confused, and he swayed a little where he stood.

"I think you had better sit down, Al," Cody recommended.

Feeling light headed, Al nodded and sat down on the scanner bed, mumbled some incoherent things the doctor couldn't make out and passed out, or crashed. Whatever the case might be, the news was too much for anybody, and Al shut down.

Later, Al asked Cody, "How long was I asleep?"

"About thirty minutes. That is how long it takes to reboot all your systems. I watched each of them come back online with the scanner. It was fascinating. If you don't mind my saying, you are a very sophisticated machine."

"This is a dream...or a nightmare. It can't be real," groaned Al.

"I am afraid it is real my friend. I have even tried pinching *myself.* It hurts."

"You're playing a joke on me, right Doc?" Al hoped.

"I wish that were so. You can see for yourself what is inside you."

Al remembered protests on Earth and laws that were passed, "Aren't humanoid robots banned on Earth?"

"Yes—they are. I did hear rumors that development was secretly still going on. I did not believe the research had gotten this far. Now I believe because here you are."

This revelation was going to take a while to sink in. At this point, Al wasn't sure what to think. He needed to get back to his routine and get busy or go crazy.

"We can't tell anybody. There must be a reason there is no mention of Al Clark in the computer and why nobody remembers me but Captain Effinger."

"You are my friend...regardless of what you are. I will say nothing," promised his friend and confidante.

"Thank you, Cody, because I have a feeling I might need all the friends I can get."

Doc Cody cleaned and wrapped his leg. He admitted he did not know how much it would help. The technology used to create Al's body was way outside of his expertise. They could only hope his leg would heal itself.

He left Cody at the clinic and took a walk around the perimeter fence to clear his head.

I think—therefore, I am, came to him.

I felt sorrow when Rudy was killed and feel affection for my friends.

Can a robot have feelings?

I don't feel strong or fast like a robot should. I don't f-e-e-l like a robot.

Does a robot know it's a robot?

Shouldn't I be able to tell?

So many questions circled in his mind with nowhere to turn for answers—or was there? The captain seemed to know more than he let on. Maybe he knew about this. If Al asked the right questions, he might get some answers. One thing was for sure. He had to be careful, and no one should know that didn't need to. It was possible even the captain was against humanoid robots.

He thought of his need for sleep. He had dreams.

Do robots dream? Al didn't know. It was all very confusing.

He decided to talk to the only robot he knew well—Robot Nine. At least, a robot could not lie, or hate. It was late, and most of the colonists were asleep when he summoned the mechanical with his pad and met the machine near some secluded equipment on the south side of camp.

Al was not sure how to start. "Robot Nine...am I human?"

"Yes sir, you are a human."

The answer surprised Al. "Am I a robot?"

"Yes sir, you are a...robot."

"Which is it?" he pressed.

"My sensors tell me you are both human and robotic."

"Please explain yourself."

"You have a human brain organ and a robotic body, sir. Does this cause you discomfort? I sense conflict in you."

"You have no idea."

"If my answers cause you discomfort, why do you ask harmful questions?"

"Because I need to know who I am. I guess that's the human part of me." Al continued, "What are my capabilities?"

"I have no data on your capabilities, sir."

Disappointed the little robot didn't know more, Al sank into thought.

"Can we discuss security details, sir, I do not wish to cause you further harm."

This one-time rogue robot seemed to possess a need to please him.

Do robots have needs?

****

CAPTAIN TOBIAS EFFINGER was extremely busy, and he didn't like it. He didn't think he should be. The captain wanted to be flying shuttle missions and helping the colony.

In this stage of their mission, it should be routine maintenance and preparation for planetfall. The discovery of the dinosaurs on Avalon complicated things, but this ship and the people on board were equipped to handle almost anything. He understood that the vessel was their home for forty-something years. Still, they should be shutting things down as the colonists left for the planet, and preparing the ship to perform settlement operations.

However, things seemed to keep going wrong on his ship.

The first problem was the air scrubbers for the hangar bay. Somehow the scrubber panels had been reversed in their slots. When people started passing out, the mistake was found and corrected. The simple error could have resulted in a grave disaster, and the captain was angry that someone as well trained as his people could allow it to happen at all.

Then the hangar bay door started acting up. It began opening to space without the force field in place; which should never occur. If not for the quick thinking of a ship engineer, the door's unprotected opening could have led to decompression of the hangar bay and a serious disaster. Until they could upgrade the security protocols, he was forced to post a guard on the door controls. They could not let it happen again.

The captain was currently at the medical center talking to the staff. People were getting sick, and the doctors were saying the water in the habitat ring was the cause.

"There is something in the water?" asked the captain of the senior MD.

"Yes, sir, the analysis we did showed a high level of contamination. Something was added; to make it toxic. The system has numerous types of filters that would have caught it, so we think the poison was put in after the filters. Someone did this on purpose Captain."

He was astonished this could happen on his ship. In all his years of service, he had never had to deal with sabotage. "Secure all access to that system after the filters; bolt it, weld it, do whatever it takes, but get it done. Are my people still in danger?"

"We have flushed the system, sir. That should take care of it." was the quick reply.

Too many problems in a short period. He had to assume they might be related. Captain Effinger left the medical center and headed back to the bridge with his assistant. There were over seven hundred souls on board, and someone appeared to be working against them.

In the captain's cabin attached to the bridge, the onboard head of security recommended they increase patrols to every half hour and concentrate on critical systems. The captain agreed, and added, "I know there are only four of you aboard. Still, I need you to begin an investigation into each incident. Advise all senior officers of the investigations, and ask for their assistance. They may know something that could be useful.

"We need to go through everyone's personnel files looking for anomalies. Recruit help from other departments if you have to. Do you understand?"

The security man looked uncomfortable, and replied, "Yes sir."

"We need to find this person, and quickly. Get to it."

Finally alone, he could take some time to think. He was starting a search of his own on his terminal when his data pad chimed. The radio technician reported, "Call from Chief Clark, sir,"

"Put it through please." When the line cleared, he said, "This is the captain."

"Hello Captain, Chief Clark here. I need to speak with you, sir."

"Well, go ahead son."

"No sir, I need to speak with you in person. I would like to arrange a meeting."

"Is something wrong Chief?" The captain didn't like the way this conversation was sounding.

"No sir—it's personal. I have a few questions about myself that I hope you can help me with."

Now the captain was concerned. "One of the shuttles is returning tomorrow, is that soon enough? Contact me when you get aboard the *Excalibur,* and we can talk. Are you sure you can't tell me what this is about?"

On the other end, Al was aching to blurt it out. One question would do it.

Am I a robot? Unfortunately, he could trust no one right now except Doc Cody.

"No sir...I'm sure. See you tomorrow. Have a good evening."

"I'm looking forward to seeing you, Mister Clark."

"Thank you, sir." Al closed the circuit feeling hopeful. The captain knew more than he was saying; how much more was anyone's guess, but he knew...something.

The captain had been dreading this day for some time. Ever since Al failed to recognize him when they met after his awakening, he knew something was wrong. He might have to be the one to tell a man he was not entirely human. It was just a matter of time before Mister Clark figured it out. He assumed something must have happened that gave it away.

The captain was also excited. If Al were to become aware of his capabilities, and learned to use them constructively, he could become one of the most valuable assets available. The problem was his information will be very unsettling for Al, and quite possibly dangerous.

****

AL HAD FOUR HOURS SLEEP when he got up and went to breakfast. He decided on a light breakfast even though he wasn't especially hungry. This was going to be a long day, and he wanted to start with a full stomach. Besides, he was not tired. A dull ache throbbed in his head which slowly diminished as the morning progressed. The shuttle wasn't leaving for another two hours, so he went to the mess hall and ordered an egg, grabbed an orange juice, and took his breakfast to a table.

It didn't look like anybody suspected he was different. He felt different. *Is Al Clark my name? Why can't I remember?* Questions bounced around in his head.

He was trying to convince himself there were good things about being robotic. He would live as long as his brain did. *That's good, right?* He should be stronger. *Why am I not stronger? Why am I eating?* His confused state of mind preoccupied him as he ate his breakfast; sitting alone, watching all the humans go about their business.

The shuttle left on time and arrived at the *Excalibur* on schedule. It was always inspiring to see the great ship in space, and to appreciate the scale of the starship as they approached. The ship was an amazing accomplishment and a tribute to the human race. He was a little surprised to find it felt good to be back.

They met in the captain's cabin for lunch. When Al arrived, he was escorted directly to his cabin. It was just the two of them at the long table, and the captain seemed a little—uneasy.

"Please have a seat, Mister Clark. I believe we're having cheeseburgers this afternoon, or what passes for cheeseburgers these days. I'll be glad when we get some real cows in a pasture. Packaged food and vegetables only go so far for me."

Al pulled out a chair and sat down at the table laid out with a formal setting.

"Thank you for seeing me so quickly sir; I know you've been really busy. They briefed me on the situation aboard ship. Any leads on the saboteur yet?"

The leader of the colony rearranged his place setting, looking down as if thinking.

"Nothing that's panned out yet. Now, what's this all about Mister Clark?"

The captain had gotten directly to the point, and Al was not yet sure how to start. What he asked next could be the moment of truth or a colossal mistake. He liked the captain and wanted to trust him, but should he dip in a toe, or jump in feet first. He was tired of mysteries. He dove in.

"Did you know I was...artificial?"

Captain Effinger took a deep breath, checked his place setting again, then looked him in the eye and said, "Yes Al, I did."

"You've known all this time?"

The captain visibly tensed and with more than a little guilt he answered Al's question. "Since I received the order to allow you on board. A month before we left. I have a book that came with you that is way over my head. However, to the right person, I'm sure it explains a lot."

After a pause, he continued, "You have the most advanced robotic body ever created—or at least, it was forty years ago."

"Why didn't you tell me? I've been going crazy trying to figure this out."

"I was ordered from the beginning to keep your secret. Most people wouldn't understand that you are a human with a robot body, they would only see you as a robot; disguised as a human. I am truly sorry, Al. Maybe I should have told you."

"Is my name Al Clark?"

The captain took a sip of his wine and chuckled, "That is the name the technical assistants gave you. They thought it was clever. The name on your compartment door actually said ALARM CLOCK. How you got Al Clark out of that, I don't know...but you were close. You were supposed to be our backup if the computer failed and were to wake us up if all else failed. It worked too—only ten years later than we planned."

A Porter stuck his head through the door and asked if they were ready to start dinner. The captain said, "Yes, of course, come on in." While the Porter was with them, they lapsed into silence, both thinking thoughts of their own.

The cheeseburgers were good. Al couldn't remember ever eating one even though the taste was familiar. Somewhere in his past, he had liked cheeseburgers and still did.

While Al ate several more questions came to mind, and he voiced one, "Why do I eat and drink? My robot body doesn't need it...does it?"

"Your body runs on a power pack inside your chest. Your brain and the outer layer of your skin, however, are organic and require nutrition and fluids. You get that by eating and drinking. Though you need less than most people do," the captain explained.

His cheeseburger was only half eaten when Al found he'd lost interest in it. He was already full. *The captain was right; he did seem to eat less than other people.* He pushed himself back from the table, leaned back in the chair, and picked his next question.

"Do I need sleep?"

"Your brain needs sleep, but there again not as much as other people."

"Why can't I remember anything before my...awakening?" Al wasn't sure if he woke up or was turned on.

Captain Effinger answered, "Now there I can't help you. The first time we met, before departure, you knew precisely who you were. You volunteered for this you see. The paperwork I received said you were in a bad accident and left without the use of your arms or legs. They offered to give you a new body and a ticket on the Excalibur, and you jumped at it. You were excited and counted the days until departure. I don't know what happened."

What the captain said made Al feel better. His life had apparently taken a turn for the worse, and when they offered him a chance for a better life he had accepted. Now he wanted to know more about the benefits of that decision. "What's good about his robot body? I don't seem to be unusually strong or that much faster than an average person. Do you know why?"

"The roboticist that designed your body, a Doctor Hawthorn, told me your body was locked in a *human simulation* mode until conditions allowed the setting to be overridden or changed. They didn't want you drawing unnecessary attention to yourself."

Al thought it might be nice to meet his creator, "I would sure love to talk to that guy."

"Hawthorn *was* aboard. He went through a lot to get a pass and accompany you. Unfortunately, he died before we could wake him...sorry. I've done some checking, though, and there is a roboticist aboard that was familiar with Doctor Hawthorn's work. He's someone you might want to talk to."

"What's his name?" asked Al.

There was a twinkle in Tobias' eye as he answered, "His name is Edward Florida. I should warn you—he is quite a character."

The captain's smile grew. "He works in the robot repair shop, and I think he can fix you up."

"That's funny, sir," Al replied half-heartedly. "I have some coordinating to do with my officers about your investigations and won't be leaving until tomorrow, so I think I will look him up."

The captain and the security chief spent another hour talking about the situations both on board the ship, and down on the planet. Al asked if he needed more men to find the saboteur, and the captain declined, believing Al needed the men he had.

By the time they parted company, Al was feeling better. It was the most enlightening afternoon of Al's life—that he could remember.

****

AL WANTED TO SPEND some time with his friends while on board and made his way to Elizabeth and Chris' quarters to finish the evening. Al was struggling with whether or not he should tell them, and was stepping through the airlock into the yellow section when the lights flickered, and then went out.

For a few seconds, everything stopped. Total silence joined the absolute dark until the emergency lights stuttered, flashed, and relit the corridor. In the distance came the sound of running footsteps, and the world restarted; quickly winding up to full speed.

Elizabeth was running down the corridor toward him. Right before she reached him, the ship jumped, followed by the sound of a distant explosion. *That's not good.*

"What's going on Liz?"

The racing woman used him to break her forward momentum and slid to a stop. She took a moment to catch her breath and exclaimed, "We have a fire in the habitat ring's main power room in the blue section. That sound was an explosion, and we need to get there fast."

Any fire on a spaceship can be a ticket to disaster. In such a contained space, if the flames didn't get you, the smoke would. There is also the risk of breaching the hull and rapid decompression. Fires created fear on a spaceship.

They worked their way through the airlock and ran down the orange section to the blue access airlock. The closer they got, the more people they saw going the opposite direction towards safety. Liz and Al did not have that option. She was the senior electrical engineer, and he was responsible for ship security. This problem was their job.

The air around the airlock was smoky, and they had to force their way through the people leaving to wait for the doors to cycle, then push their way into the blue section. The blue corridor on the other side of the airlock was thick with black smoke.

"The power room is at the end of the passageway by the number three spoke," Liz told him in-between coughs. They made it halfway to the room before she collapsed onto the floor and passed out.

Al could barely see, but he picked her up and rushed back to the airlock and handed her to the last of the evacuees. He pointed to one of them and said, "Give me your shirt. I need something to wrap around my face." He held the man's shirt up to his mouth and went back to try again.

He ran to the other end of the corridor and realized the shirt was not needed. He seemed to be breathing just fine. When he reached the power room, he found all three airtight doors standing wide open, blocked from closing. *That is not supposed to happen.*

He crouched as he entered the room, and tried to discover the reason for the smoke and alarms. In the middle of the chamber, a console of large circuit breakers was engulfed in flames. Al knew the fire system couldn't operate with the doors open. If he can close the doors, it might activate the system and allow it to extinguish the fire.

Al crawled to the nearest door and gave it a solid push. Nothing happened. It was getting increasingly difficult to see, and the reason it wouldn't close was hard to determine. He pushed again—only with more force. Something popped at the bottom of the door, and it reluctantly closed. He pushed firmly on the other two open barriers, and they too swung shut.

He slipped out of the room as the last door closed, and was relieved to see the fire system activate and empty the room of air. Fans came on in the corridor, and the air began to clear. As fast as it started, the crisis ended.

He hurried down the hallway entering living quarters looking for casualties. Inside the door of one apartment, he found a little girl lying on the floor unconscious. Quickly, he picked her up and carried her to the airlock.

When he walked out of the airlock, all smoky and dirty holding that little girl, the entire corridor full of people burst into applause. The parents took her and were standing there in tears, thanking him over and over. Al thought, *that worked out well, and nobody suspects I am more than I appear.*

A much recovered Liz took his arm as they left the crowd, and she walked him to her quarters. She left him to recover and get cleaned up while she returned to assess the damage. Chris was there when they arrived, and she filled him in on Al's heroic deeds before she grabbed a flashlight and left.

Chris asked, "Are you okay?"

"I'm all right; there wasn't much to it,"

"Not according to my mother. She made it sound like you saved the day."

"Really, Chris, it was nothing."

The young man was aware they had a saboteur, and it raised a logical question, "How do you think it started?"

Al told him what he discovered. "Someone blocked all the doors open and set a fire. It was sabotage—no doubt about it. We need to catch this guy before he starts killing people."

"He already has. A girl died a little while ago from drinking the water. She was only twelve years old."

While Al was saving one girl, another had died.

He was getting angry, and he didn't understand how anyone could hurt people on purpose. "I need to get back to the scene of the fire and see if I can help."

He got up and went to the kitchen to clean up. Chris went to Al's quarters to get him some clean clothes and half an hour later, Al was going back to the power room to talk with his men already there. His problems would have to wait.

The power room looked bad. Liz told him it would have been a lot worse if he had not put the fire out. She was busy reading schematics on her pad, throwing switches, and resetting breakers to try to reroute and restore power. It was a high voltage primary breaker that exploded, and the debris was strewn everywhere.

His men were off to the side using their pads to review the camera video from the room before the fire started, and they got lucky. The person responsible had known where all the cameras were—except one. This one camera recorded a slight figure in a big hurry to weld the doors open. At one point, the figure looked around, and they got a full view of the face. It was the face of a woman. *Why do people automatically assume saboteurs are men?*

"Run that through the computer and see if we can get a name," Al instructed.

One of them exclaimed, "I think I know her, she works in the shuttle bay on the night shift. She's a bit of a loner that stays to herself, but I always thought she was just shy. We should talk to her."

"We were just given a gift, gentlemen. A clear image of the person that blocked those doors, and probably started the fire. Let's not waste our gift. Please, let's get this done, I would like to talk to this person within the hour. Let me know when you have her in custody." They hesitated, and he reiterated, "Go on—get going."

Liz was leaning over a bank of breakers close to where the fire had been and was pulling on something. Al walked over to assist.

"Need some help?"

Liz looked up and smiled, "As a matter of fact, I can't get this panel to break loose."

"Here, let me see." Al reached over and saw her hand on a handle. "It pulls straight out?"

"It's supposed to."

Al grabbed the handle and carefully pulled, trying not to have it fly out and bounce against the wall; he increased the pressure until it broke loose and slid open.

"You are my hero for the second time today. I should ask you to dinner or something," she suggested.

"Sorry, but I still have things to do. I'll take a rain check, though."

Liz got an inquisitive look on her face, "What did you and the captain talk about?"

"I think it's top secret. Need to know and all that."

She laughed, "I'll get it out of you, just not right now. I have to get the power back on."

"Need anything else?"

"No, I'm good. I should be finished here in an hour or two. Maybe I'll see you then?"

With regret, Al replied, "I don't think I'll have time tonight, and I go back to the surface in the morning. I expect to be interrogating the person that did this shortly. Maybe we can stop this lunacy before it gets any worse."

"I hope you can stop it before more people get killed. If you come up here again before I come down, give me a call."

They said their goodbyes and Al left to head for the security office. A couple of people acknowledged him on his way and shook his hand, saying things like, "Way to go Chief." and "Nice job." He was embarrassed and dismissive. He didn't think of himself as a hero. Still, he had to admit it *did* feel good.

****

WHEN THEY BROUGHT HER in, she was small like Ana, but not like Ana. This girl did not have the advantages that Ana had been born with, and it showed in her demeanor. Her name was Tammy Shoemaker, and she was a young girl under twenty; now a scared and fidgety bird in a trap.

Tammy hid her fear with anger at the officers that held her arms and guided her to the holding cell, cursing at them with a wicked tongue.

"Let me go you **** planet stealers! I don't care what the hell you do to me; I will tell you nothing because I have done nothing wrong."

Al watched from his desk without saying a word, trying to get a handle on how to deal with her. They put her in the cell and locked the door, leaving her alone and in a lot of trouble.

"Let me out of here. I haven't done anything. I demand you let me go."

She suddenly realized that they did not particularly care what she had to say. The look in their eyes told her they didn't care for her at all. She threw herself onto the bunk and sat there in defiance; trying unsuccessfully to hide her fear.

Tammy had long brown hair and a pixie face with a turned up nose and green eyes. She had on the dirty uniform of a maintenance worker that did little to hide a small, slender frame.

"Where did you find her," Al asked his officer.

"She was in her quarters sir, getting ready to take a shower. I think we surprised her. There was a portable welding set-up in her closet and some chemical containers that she could have added to the water. They are analyzing it now. Fingerprints and DNA are also in the process."

Al, the man responsible for all the settlers' safety, watched his prisoner. He continued to keep his eyes on her as he grabbed a chair, set it down backward in front of the cell, and wrapped his arms around the seatback. The girl had grown quiet and was staring at the floor.

She must realize they would charge her with endangering the lives of all on board—and possibly murder. What would make someone do something like this?

Al sat watching her for a while in thought. He forced a reasonable tone into his voice and asked, "When a crazy person does something especially nuts, the one question normal people are left with is—why? Why would you do this?"

She hesitated for a second and then raised her head. Defiantly she exclaimed, "I am not crazy. I am here to stop you. You have no right to steal someone else's planet. You ruin your own world, and then build big ships to go out and destroy other people's worlds. This mission is what I was destined to give my life for, and I only wish I was better at it."

Al was stunned. He did not need to ask more questions. The hatred apparent on her face made him believe this girl was likely the product of highly radicalized thinking. What kind of life must she have endured for her to think as she does?

It struck him that she might be a victim of chance; wrong place, wrong time, and the wrong people. Al's anger turned to frustration when he realized her misguided beliefs might not be entirely her fault. These were the twisted views of humans that taught terrorism, and a fervent cause, put forth properly, can become overwhelming. Punishing her would change nothing.

He decided to change his tactics. "Are you hungry, or thirsty?"

"I could use a plate of freedom."

"Sorry, can't do that. You'll stay where you are until we can figure out what to do with you."

Al stood up and returned the chair to its place by the desk. He motioned to Sid, the senior officer, to move out of the girl's hearing and told him, "Sid, I want you to make sure she gets some psychiatric help. That is one mixed up kid. I'm going to file a report for the captain but make sure you keep him up-to-date, okay?"

"Will do Chief. Have a safe trip tomorrow."

Al went back to his compartment. It was late, and he was tired. Even though he didn't need as much sleep as other people, he needed it now. Tomorrow would be a whole new day for him, and he wanted to be at his best. In the morning, he had one more stop to make before he rode the shuttle back to Avalon. He wanted to talk to the robot expert.

****

THAT NIGHT AL HAD THE dream again. The same recurring dream that always ended at the same point. He was standing on a grassy hill looking down on a village, with a person running towards him yelling something he couldn't quite understand.

He woke up confused, with the images fresh in his mind, and then the dream faded away, leaving only small snippets of the whole. There were, however, fragments that remained in his memory. He remembered it made him happy.

Al left his quarters early and made his way directly to the hangar bay where the robotics repair shop was located. He approached the door to the sound of music. Inside, a group was performing an old song Al found vaguely familiar—something about a silver hammer.

He entered the room and closed the door behind him. The music was loud, and the smell of oil and plastic permeated the shop. A short, wild-haired man stood on a table with one of the gardening robots lying beneath him. He was singing along with the band and preparing to swing a large silver hammer at its round silver head when Al interrupted, "Hey...it looks to me like he gave up."

The white haired man jumped and turned to determine where the voice came from, "Well...hello there, Sheriff. I wasn't expecting anybody this early. Grab a seat; I'll be right with you."

Al watched as he set his hammer down and climbed down from the table. Short, and older, he was a man of fifty or so, with an energetic face, unruly long white hair, and bright blue eyes. He wore a long white coat with more than a few oily stains.

The roboticist went to a small tablet and turned his music down, wiped his hands with a cloth, and walked over to where Al was standing. His coat had a name tag on it that said, Dr. Edward Florida.

"I hope you don't misunderstand what I was doing just then," he asked. "To remove that robot's head you have to strike a particular spot with sufficient force to dislodge it from the body. I find it easier to be overhead." He offered his hand and said, "Pleasure to meet you, Mister Clark."

As they shook hands, Al asked, "You know who I am?"

"Everyone knows who Chief Al Clark is. You're making quite a name for yourself in our little community. My understanding is you've already saved several lives. Is that not so?"

"I was lucky enough to be in the right place at the right time. I think fortune smiled on me," was Al's humble reply.

"Nevertheless, Mister Clark, you are well known in these parts and highly respected. What can I do for you this fine day?"

Al considered how to continue. He needed someone who knew about the human brain and robot combination, and someone versed in this field that could decipher the manual the captain possessed. Still, he needed to be discreet.

Al replied, "You too, Doctor Florida, are also highly respected. I've done a little checking on you, and learned you are both a doctor and a roboticist; regarded by some to be one of the best in both fields. Can I ask why it is that you are down here, in the back end of the ship repairing maintenance robots?"

Doctor Florida chuckled, "If you mean *why* I am here on this vessel, it's because robotics became too restrictive on Earth. I have interests they did not appreciate. If you mean why I am *here* repairing robots, it's because somebody has to care for them and I enjoy it. Does that answer your question, Mister Clark?"

A little chagrined, Al continued, "I'm told you are familiar with Dr. Hawthorn's work. Is this true?"

The doctor recognized the name immediately and was quick to answer, "Doctor Hawthorn was a genius, a dreamer, and a revolutionary. The combination of which leads to amazing discoveries. He was a visionary when it came to robotics. What a tragedy it is that he didn't live to see our new world."

"So I take it you approved of his work?"

"Oh yes, he was doing some extraordinary work on human integration to robotic constructs. Unfortunately, it was highly controversial, and they revoked his funding. That is the reason he joined our expedition. He hoped to continue his research here, and I was hoping to collaborate with him."

"Are you doing research of your own in that area?" Al asked.

"I was...but there hasn't been much free time. Maybe later, once we are settled."

Al made his decision to get some professional help. They were alone in the small room. Several closed doors led to other areas in the shop. Just to be sure, he leaned up close to the roboticist's ear and asked, "Can you keep a secret?"

Doctor Florida said he could, and Al told him his story in an abbreviated form, starting with waking up in the box and ending with his experience in the power room.

The roboticist was surprised—and then delighted. "You are the prototype?"

"In the flesh, so to speak," Al answered.

Doctor Florida was not so surprised that he didn't think to run some tests. As a roboticist, Al was like finding the Holy Grail.

"Let's go into the diagnostic room so I can examine you."

He asked Al to sit on a table and knelt down to look at his wounded leg.

"This is healing nicely, in a couple of weeks you won't be able to tell it was injured," predicted the doctor.

It took them several minutes to figure out how to open the access panel located on Al's back. A tiny mole pressed just the right way opened a small panel, and allowed the roboticist to hook up his equipment.

"Ah...ha, now we're getting somewhere," he exclaimed happily while he grabbed leads and plugged them into the proper ports of the scanner and Al's back. A large monitor burst into life and displayed the workings of Al's body in exquisite detail. Rods and tubes, servos and motors, things that Al had no idea of their purpose, and miles of intricate wiring. Lines of code, parameters, and status, scrolled down both sides of the digital representation of his body.

The doctor and scientist turned to Al and said, "Now that is a thing of beauty. Simple and elegant. No disrespect intended."

"None taken Doc...is everything all right? Do I need a charge or anything?" Al asked; unsure of himself.

"Everything is fine Chief Clark. See how your leg is getting extra fluids to help it regenerate the skin structure. I know your power pack is good for many years in the *human* mode, and it appears you are eating and drinking enough to maintain your biological aspects. No, I would say your body is fine, but how about the mental portion of your well-being? Are you sleeping well? Any depression or anxiety?"

"It's been getting better since I found out what I am. In the beginning, it was kind of scary," admitted Al.

"From what I've heard, I would say you're adapting well to a challenging and frightening situation. You mentioned a manual the captain has. Can I get my hands on that?"

Doctor Florida was licking his lips and rubbing his hands. Begging to know Al and his robotic body better.

Al grinned at the image this mad scientist looking man made and answered him, "I will ask the captain to get it to you. You must remember, though, for the time being...tell no one. The captain, Doctor Cody, and you are the only ones that know. If anyone else needs to become involved, I should be the one to tell them. Do you agree?"

"Absolutely. There are people in this camp that would not take kindly to having a cybernetic person among them. For you to help the colonists, you must be liked by them. I totally understand why you want to keep your identity secret. In a different time, I'd tell you to wear a mask." Edward Florida thought that was funny. "You could be the first superhero of Avalon." The look he gave Al was one of mischief, and then he laughed.

Al had a bigger question, "What happens when you take me out of *human* mode?"

"At this point, I'm not sure. I assume your strength and speed would increase substantially. There is a possibility your senses will be better. I will know more after I get a look at Dr. Hawthorn's manual. However, I don't recommend you change that setting too soon. We need to do some systems tests and psychological evaluations. Let's take it slow and work up to your full potential in baby steps. I'm not sure you realize this yet, but...you can be a very dangerous man."

Chapter Fifteen

The shuttle floated down from the clouds to an expanding settlement. A lot had happened to him in only one day. If you add the problems he experienced last night, it seemed much longer.

When Al stepped from the shuttle, there were one-hundred and three people working on-planet to make this place their home. Activity surrounded him as the colonists rushed to get settled.

It was late afternoon, and the sun was casting long shadows across the security office when he arrived. Large windows in each wall provided plenty of light for their needs. Behind a curtain, four bunks filled half the habitat, with two tables and accompanying chairs filling the rest of the small office. Two of his men were sitting in chairs staring at two pads propped up on a table. Another officer returned in the same shuttle as Al and left for lunch. The rest were sleeping behind the curtain or out on patrol.

The two men at the table were seeing through the Watcher's eyes; reading the data their sensors generated. They were responsible for the vigil against dragons.

"Have you seen anything?" their boss asked.

The man closest to Al took his eyes from the security pad and answered, "There was a smaller creature like the ones that attacked us, throwing rocks at a fence post just before dawn. He didn't do any damage, but he had us going for a while."

"Watcher one saw two giant long-necked creatures from a distance an hour ago. It was triggered by the noise and gave us twenty seconds of video. Want to see it?"

"Sure, these are our neighbors. We should learn all we can."

The video was sharp and clear and showed two giant creatures with long thin necks two miles away, lumbering across the screen. They reminded him of pictures from a book; a book about Earth's distant past.

"I don't think they are interested in us. Still, I'm glad they're way out there." Al remarked. "Keep your eyes open. I'm going on a walkabout and talk to you guys later."

A walkabout is what they now referred to as their informal patrols. They just walked—about. Al left the office and went to grab something to eat. He had not eaten anything since last night, and although his stomach could not growl, he felt his hunger as a fuzziness of thought that progressively got worse.

The mess hall was a large tent until they completed the permanent building. Al picked up his dinner and was sitting by himself at a table when Cody came in, looked around until he saw Al, and made his way over.

"There you are," he said, "How are you doing my friend?"

"I'm doing all right, all in all. How about you?" Al replied with a little apprehension.

"I am fine...but I need to talk to you. It is extremely important. Can we go to the clinic?"

Al was almost done eating his small meal, so he threw the remains in the trash and followed the doctor out.

"What's the matter, Cody?"

"I will show you when we get there."

They arrived at the clinic and went directly to the diagnostic room. Cody locked the door and then pulled up Al's scan on the monitor.

He turned and said, "You have a hole in your head."

"Umm...excuse me?"

Doctor Cody tapped the monitor and zoomed in on the forehead. He pointed to a tiny dot. A dot on *his* forehead.

"That is a hole in the metal of your head. My scan cannot penetrate the metal surrounding your brain, so I cannot see inside, but the scan shows a tiny hole. Are you feeling all right? Do you remember banging your head?"

Then it came to him. Al remembered a foggy mirror in a vacant and unused bathroom and a tiny drop of blood on his forehead. He remembered a pinhole when he woke up—in the lid of his box, and the holes in the habitat ring made from micro-meteorites. He thought of the dull headaches he'd begun to have.

Al mentioned all this to his friend and voiced his concern. "Is it possible I have a meteorite fragment in my head?"

His friend looked worried, "It might be. We will need to do more tests."

"What should we do?" asked Al.

"Did you see the roboticist while you were aboard the Excalibur? Did he do a scan?"

"I did see him, and he performed a scan."

"The download from his scan might tell us if you are in danger. His equipment is more sophisticated and can give us more detail."

Cody thought for a few seconds and considered the dangers involved with exposing Al's secret to the settlement, "I must go and see him myself. We cannot trust the radio, so I must take a shuttle up to the ship. I will leave tomorrow morning and be back the next day. Until I return, you must promise me you will take it easy...yes?"

Al had many questions. The one that jumped out immediately was, "Do you think this might be the reason for my amnesia?"

"I think it is a distinct possibility, my friend."

****

IT WAS DARK OUTSIDE when he left the clinic. The settlement lights lit up the night. Still, many areas were left in dark shadow. Most colonists were inside for supper or doing preparations for the next day's work, and the colony had grown quiet.

Al was in a mild state of shock. His life was once again in chaos, and he was unsure of his future. His headache was gone, and he felt fine, but he was not happy. Waiting for Doc Cody to return was going to be difficult.

The night was the time of monsters. Al and his men had adopted the local name for the beasts, and when the sun went down, they knew the 'Riktors' would be hunting. While four of his people were patrolling the camp, two more monitored the feed coming from the Watchers. Sleep was something done during the day.

He decided to walk the fence and check the installation. He wanted to make sure it was working as intended. Al stopped by the security office and informed his men. Then he grabbed a powerful flashlight and a rifle—just in case one of the monsters was stupid enough to try something—and he left. His mood was such that he almost wished they would try something.

Walking the fence was therapeutic. Insects buzzed, and animals called to each other in voices of their own. The noises of the night reminded him of Earth on a pleasant spring evening. There were large versions of fireflies that dotted the landscape, their tails blinking as they made lazy circles in the air. If it weren't for the occasional animal scream or savage growl in the distance, it would have been more relaxing.

The perimeter posts that generated the fence were designed to stun. Now and then his flashlight would spotlight some creature that attempted to pass through the invisible barrier. The paralyzing effect started at the bottom and got progressively stronger until it reached the ten-foot level. Sometimes, a creature stunned by the fence would wake up a half-hour later and go the wrong way; paralyzing themselves again.

In one section Al found evidence of a large animal that tried the fence, smashing some small bushes and leaving the ground marked with the fall of its body. Further down, he found another spot where it attempted to break through again. *This creature is persistent.*

When he reached the part of the perimeter furthest from the main camp and its lights, in the darkest part of the line of fence poles, he found a hole dug under the fence. A rather large hole dug hurriedly since sunset. Claw tracks led away from the hole, headed in the direction of Camelot.

"We have an intruder," Al announced over the radio. "The southwest corner fence has been compromised, and tracks lead inbound. If it is a Riktor, remember—they may hunt in pairs. I am making my way in from the compromised section of the fence."

He could hear his men commanding everyone to get to the habitats as he followed the tracks toward town.

In a tent next to a half-finished habitat module, he heard someone screaming. His flashlight beam lit the back of an angry monster, at least eight foot tall, dragging a woman out through a tear in the tent. He had her by the legs with his front claws and was pulling her from the safety of her home. She was kicking and screaming and doing her best to make his intentions difficult.

Al looked around for an accomplice and didn't see one. It appeared to be alone. He yelled, "Hey—over here!" It was crucial he get the creature away from the woman. A man ran out through the tent flap and helped to distract the determined Riktor, and to his credit, the man was a fast runner.

The monster turned his attention to Al. One of his officers appeared twenty feet to his side and followed the Chief's example. In a rage, the beast looked back and forth trying to decide which human to attack. Both men began moving backward, attempting to draw it away from the tent and the victim.

The Riktor dropped the woman, and she jumped up and ran to safety. Then it started moving towards them roaring his displeasure. As the creature moved out, the two men circled slowly around to get a clear line of fire. When the time was right, Al screamed, "Fire!"

The monster was no match for the laser rifles; set to maximum; they almost cut him in half. His final roar died in his throat, and he fell hard to the ground.

Al was running over to check on the woman when the second Riktor exploded from behind a neighboring habitat not twenty feet away. With an ear-splitting roar, it thundered toward Al. He had no time to think. There was nothing else he could do but let instinct take over, and he fell onto his back to the dirt. The surprised beast flew over him, and the beam from Al's rifle opened it up. The first monster's partner dropped to the dirt in a heap behind him.

That is how Al got his fourth Riktor. He was a hero to the colonists—again, and now a mortal enemy of the surviving beasts.

****

IT WASN'T LONG AFTER the battle that his headache returned. It started at annoying and moved towards just bearable within an hour. Eventually, it progressed to the point where he was forced to excuse himself and went to lie down. In the security quarters, he dropped into one of the bunks and promptly fell asleep.

The dream was incredibly real this time. Al could smell the grass, hear the wind, and see for miles over the bright and beautiful countryside. The person running up the hill was still fuzzy. As she got closer her dress turned blue, and she looked vaguely familiar. Whatever it was she was trying to tell him never became clear enough to understand.

Al awoke six hours later with only a trace of the pain, and bright sunshine shone through glowing orange curtains. Al did not move right away; contemplating his headache and the reason behind it. He concluded stress made his headaches worse, and it was something he needed to avoid. He got up hoping he could catch Cody before he left and let him know about the newest developments.

The doctor was already gone when Al reached the shuttle pads, and he told himself it was just as well. Doc Cody looked worried enough when he last saw him.

Al opted to stay busy. There were fences that needed reinforcing. He had excavators dig a ten-foot trench six inches wide between each post, and then the machine filled the channels with a fast drying polymer that dried harder than concrete. A deep tunnel would have to be dug to get under the fence, and Al supervised the entire thing.

Since the machines did most of the work, all he had to do was make sure the fence posts were not damaged. His men took responsibility for the security of the town when it became apparent Al was struggling with something.

He was finishing up and taking care of last minute details when he saw the shuttle touch down in the late afternoon the following day. Al made his way to the shuttle pad and watched as Doc Cody, followed closely by Edward Florida, stepped quickly over to Al.

Cody wasted no time with small talk and told him straight away, "You need to come back to the ship. We need to run some tests, but it appears you need surgery. Dr. Florida has detected some swelling of your brain, which is more than likely causing your headaches. We need to remove the meteoroid fragment as soon as possible."

"Are you telling me I need brain surgery?" Al had avoided considering the idea. Brain surgery was something he thought of as dangerous, painful, and with terrible odds of success.

Doctor Florida wanted somewhere more private, so they went to the clinic. Once inside, with the doors locked and the curtains drawn, his friends attempted to console him.

"It's not as bad as it sounds," said Edward. "We simply have to make an incision around the head and get access to the brain pan cover. Lift the lid, and we can then remove the meteoroid and prevent further damage."

Al did not like the sound of any of this.

He tried some humor, "I feel much better now, maybe it will go away on its own."

Cody told him, "This will only get worse, my friend."

Doc Cody was concerned and was afraid Al was running out of time. He agreed with Edward and wanted to perform the operation without delay.

Al knew he had no choice, and gave in. "All right. How will this work?"

Cody and Edward glanced at one another, each in silent agreement, and Cody explained, "We will have to perform the surgery on the ship in doctor Florida's diagnostic room. I will make the incision to open the cover, and Ed will remove the fragment. Then we just close the cover and stitch the incision. You will be right as rain in no time."

"I'm not going to walk around like Frankenstein and make grunting noises am I?"

"Now Al, you should take this seriously," pleaded Cody.

"No electricity to the temples or anything like that?"

"Al...please," begged Cody.

Al gave them a grin and said, "All right already. When do we leave?"

"Pack yourself a bag and be prepared to be gone for a week or so. We have permission to use a shuttle, and we leave in thirty minutes."

Cody turned and started filling a suitcase with what he thought he might need from the clinic. Doctor Florida studied Al's scan while Al went to pack a bag and let his men know he was leaving. He made a quick trip to his tiny sleeping quarters, and the security shack, and ten minutes later they were on the shuttle and headed to the Excalibur.

The captain met them on the hangar floor of the ship and escorted them directly to the robotics shop. "Good luck Mister Clark, just listen to the doctors and everything will be all right. Don't worry—we'll take care of everything."

He turned to Edward and asked to be kept informed, posted a guard on the outside door, and left to attend to his ship.

Inside the room, they ran some tests, and when they were ready, they had him step into a tube recessed into the floor that placed his head at shoulder height. They then filled it with a special foam that immobilized him.

Edward, the not always funny roboticist, would have put it like this. "We locked him down, opened his lid, removed a grain of metal, and closed him back up."

Not that it was quite that simple, but the operation did go pretty much according to plan. Two hours later, Al was sleeping comfortably in a recovery bed. The doctors were standing to the side discussing their friend and the operation.

"Do you think he will be okay Edward?" asked Cody.

"We never know with brain injuries. The connection to the body is complex and delicate. We can only hope he does not become worse. I don't think we did more damage, though, because the foreign matter came out so easily. I am very optimistic."

Cody asked the question Al had asked, "You are a robotic specialist and have had some time to go over Al's operational manual. Can you tell me what his capabilities will be when he recovers fully?"

With a seriousness that surprised Cody, Edward replied, "Without restrictions, he could be almost unstoppable. The documentation describes abilities far above a normal human. He could be the very thing that allows us to remain here. On the other hand, there are those that will fear him, and they may try to cause him harm."

Doctor Edward Florida *had* read the manual and had a pretty good idea what Al could do when unrestricted. What he knew of Al as a person—made him feel better about it.

****

AL CLARK WOKE UP THREE days later; if it can be called waking up. He tried to open his eyes and couldn't. He was awake; yet not awake, and could neither see nor hear anything other than an annoying ringing in his head. With no input from the outside world, Al was trapped inside his own head.

Recent memories flooded back and he remembered the surgery. *Had something gone wrong?*

Al's old friend Mister Fear knocked loudly at the door. *Was this the way it was going to be from now on—had the surgery caused him to lose the use of his body?*

Dr. Edward Florida walked into the room, looked at a monitor for a moment, flicked a couple of switches on the machine hooked to the half human, half robot, and brought Al back to the rest of the world. His machine body reconnected to his human brain, and Al was alive again.

He opened his eyes to the whisper of machines and fans flooding his ears. Standing next to him was a smiling Doctor Florida, and at the foot of his bed were the captain and Doc Cody, also smiling.

"Welcome back Mister Clark," the captain said. "You had us worried."

Al tried moving his legs to sit up and couldn't. He attempted raising his arm and had the same lack of response. "I can't move."

"Don't worry Al; I have the rest of your body shut down. I wanted your brain to get a chance to rest without the added stimulus. How do you feel?" the roboticist asked.

"A little groggy. Other than that...I feel okay. There is a buzzing in my head."

The roboticist answered, "That is probably the feedback from your body being disabled. It will go away when I restart the rest of you. Try and take it easy Al, everything is going to be fine."

"How long have I been out?"

Cody spoke up, "We have been giving you a chemical to induce sleep, and you've been asleep for three days, but everything we have seen so far points to a full recovery." With a big grin on his face, he added, "You are going to be good as gold my friend."

During his recovery, Al's friends came to see him. One or two at a time. As a cover story, they were told he had a small brain tumor that was successfully removed.

It was good to see Liz and Chris, who were happily preparing to move down to Avalon. They were excited because living on a spaceship was no comparison to living on a living, breathing planet.

Kayla and Ana came by and brought books and flowers. They too would be going down to Avalon. However, they were more scared than excited.

Kayla explained their apprehension, "You've had to kill four of those creatures. That sounds like a dangerous place to us."

"Someone told me they dragged a lady right out of her tent. Did that happen?" asked Ana.

Al shrugged and tried to reassure them. "Yes that's true, but she was only scratched. We do have some things to work out. We'll improve the fence and the overall security procedures, and the settlement will become safer. With the help of the natives, we might be able to solve the Riktor problem altogether. It's possible that after losing so many of their own, the creatures will decide we're not worth the trouble and just leave us alone."

"Do you think so?" asked Ana.

"No...It is, however, a nice thought. Don't worry you two; we will keep perfecting our defenses and find ways to keep everyone safe. Trust me."

A week went by uneventfully. Al's closest friends were his only visitors, and that was rare. Most of the time he was bored to tears. His surgery was still on a *need to know* basis, so most people had no idea what happened to him. The people on the planet were made to believe he was assigned to the ship temporarily, and the people on the ship were made to believe he was still on Avalon. Al just disappeared into the robot shop.

He spent most of his time on paperwork pertaining to his profession, listening to Edward Florida's music, and reading books. On the eighth day, he was smuggled out and returned to Camelot. The captain cleared the hangar bay, and the patient was ushered out directly onto a shuttle that took him home; landing shortly before sunrise. From there it was a short walk to the security office.

The settlement had changed considerably. It was more than a camp now and growing rapidly into a village. Dozens of habitat buildings placed beside wide sawdust sidewalks, with larger buildings under construction for common use, were being prepared for habitation. Some settlers had already started to adapt their homes to their personal preferences, and a few houses had sapling trees planted in the small front yards. To Al, it seemed an excellent beginning for the time they'd been there.

Liz suggested he wear a hat to hide his bandaged head. He had no preference, and it sounded like a nice change, so he had a cowboy hat made. He was wearing that hat when he walked into the office and surprised his deputies.

"Well howdy, Sheriff. What's with the hat?" one said with a grin.

"It's my new look, what do ya think?"

"It looks good on you, and makes you look more...Sheriffy," he said.

There were two men just finishing their overnight shift of monitoring the Watchers, two more were getting dressed, and two were preparing to go out on patrol. Robot Nine was already out checking the fence. All six men were dying to know what had happened to Al.

"I had to have a little surgery," he told them. "Everything is fine, and I'll be back to normal in a week or two." Al didn't want to get into too many details, so he told them the brain tumor story and brushed off the rest of their questions.

He sat down at the table and asked, "So...what did I miss while I was gone?"

Sid, the man in charge in his absence filled him in. "Luckily, we've had no Riktor sightings since the last attack. It seems we might have scared them off for the time being." He paused to organize his thoughts. "The twelve-year-old girl that was murdered by the saboteur was buried three days ago next to Rudy in our new cemetery. Her parents are taking it pretty hard and are demanding justice. They want to see someone hanged or electrocuted or something.

"It seems a lot of people want to know if our prisoner is responsible for our waking up ten years late. Oh,...and we have a visitor from the natives. She showed up not long after you left. Seems to be a nice kid, maybe fifteen, her name is Kira and she's staying with Cindy and Rahul. She's been walking around with

160

them and soaking up everything. I hope what she is learning does not come back to haunt us."

The Chief of Security was well aware that having her in the camp was a risk. He thought it a risk worth taking. Developing trust with their neighbors was crucial. Which meant addressing the issue of prejudice needed to begin now.

"Try not to think of it that way. We are building a new society here, and we're going to need the native's help. They know more about this planet than we will ever know, and in return, we can help them. It's important to remember this has been their home for a long time, and we need mutual trust between us if we are going to live here."

Al smiled and got off the soapbox, "How's Robot Nine. Is he working out okay?"

"He comes in here every morning asking about you. I think he missed you Chief," one man said as he walked out the door.

"Well, I think I might just look him up so he can stop worrying. And maybe see a few other people while I'm at it. You guys okay here?"

"We have it under control," they told him.

It started raining as he left, but he didn't care. He was happy to be alive, and he had his hat to keep his head dry. Things were starting to look up again.

Chapter Sixteen

Kira left early to visit the gods on the day of her appointment. She dressed in her finest furs and carried with her more of the colorful chains woven from the hair of the Minitat to give as gifts. It was easy to see the gods were pleased when the tribe presented the first necklace. The braided strings around her neck accentuated her long auburn hair, dark brown eyes, and her colorful outfit; she was a beautiful tribute.

Everyone was there to wish her good fortune. She hurried to say her goodbyes and started down the path to the Kuthra's kingdom. She did not hurry. If the gods were to sacrifice her, she wanted to treasure every moment of her life until then.

The girl, not quite considered an adult, was still dazed from being picked to be the one to visit the Kuthra. The elders wanted a young person with a sharp mind, who questioned everything. Everyone knew she was always asking questions.

Along the way she bent a tiny branch every so often to allow her people to track her if they needed to, more out of habit than conscious thought. She arrived at the gate to the Kuthra kingdom as the sun became whole on the horizon, adding a bright and colorful tint to everything she saw. Waiting for her were the two Kuthra she met at the caves, and they appeared excited to see her.

Rahul and Cindy turned off the section of fence the colony used as a gate and rushed up to her. Kira mistook their intention, took a step backward, and dropped to the ground in an attempt not to offend them.

It did not take long for the specialists to rein in their enthusiasm, convince the frightened Avalonian to stand, and introduce themselves.

One of the gods said, "Rahul," while pointed to himself. He did this several times, and then he indicated the God that accompanied him and said, "Cindy."

A smart girl, Kira quickly realized what he was trying to say. *He is telling me what to call them!*

The young native with the long dark hair indicated herself and said, "Kira," and the gods were pleased. The next few hours were like an incredible dream. She absorbed the sights and sounds, and they filled her with wonder.

The gods have homes outside the mountain; sitting open in a field. They must be very powerful not to be afraid. Boxes that move by themselves walk around and do their work for them.

What she saw was confusing and awe-inspiring—and a little frightening.

That was how her stay with the gods began, and she learned at an astounding rate. Kira was inquisitive and never hesitated to ask questions. She was also very determined to learn to speak with the gods. She wanted to know if they were the kind and powerful gods of their teachings, or something else. Her people needed them to be kind and powerful.

The gods do not need flames for cooking. They sit around open fires and do little more than admire the fires they build. Inside their houses, they would take something from a silver container, remove a thin colorful wrapper, put it back in a different box, and out would come a delicious meal. There was magic in the white sticks surrounding their kingdom that put bad things to sleep. She discovered one miracle after another.

One God spoke into a little box he held in his hand, *and tiny beings inside the box answered back—with strong voices!*

The local girl from Avalon was in heaven. Living and learning among the Gods.

****

IT WAS RAINING WHEN Al returned to see the prisoner aboard the Excalibur. For that reason, he wore his hat. The bandages were gone, but the rain wasn't. It had been raining since he walked out of the security shack a week ago, and had not stopped. They were experiencing the spring rainy season that Kira informed them happened every year. It was a warm light shower that resolutely refused to stop.

Two weeks after the surgery, he still could not remember anything more about his past than he did before. It was a possibility the doctors had mentioned and he was resolved to make the best of what he did know. He had hoped the tiny meteoroid was the cause of his amnesia and his headaches. He still couldn't remember. On the other hand, he no longer had the pain in his head or the confused thinking. He decided he could live with that.

When Al boarded the shuttle he was thinking, *maybe the meteoroid was responsible for my waking up, which allowed me to wake all the rest. It is possible that minuscule chunk of metal allowed him to save the ship, and, therefore everyone on it. There was a silver lining inside the meteor cloud.*

Tammy Shoemaker stayed locked in her cell for more than a month. Al meant to visit her sooner until life kept interfering. No one came to visit her but the officers stuck guarding her, and *they* were not happy about it. It was reported she mostly read and meditated, and honestly believed she was not long for this world, or any other.

Accompanied by two of his officers from the planet, they came to escort her down to Avalon. The *Excalibur* was being prepared for extended orbit, and most of the people were already down on the planet. Soon, the ship would have only a skeleton crew.

She was to have a trial, by a jury of her peers. Even on a colony ship, there is a need for lawyers, and one of them was assigned to represent her. The security team was there to move her to the temporary jail at Camelot—to prepare for the trial.

Al moved a chair over to the cell and asked, "How are you, Tammy?"

Her reply was blunt. "I'm all right...for a dead person."

"Now why do you say that?"

"I know what happens to people that don't conform to your principles." She made this statement with conviction; sure of her fate.

"It hasn't been decided what will happen to you. You will have to go through a trial."

"There is not a person on this ship that will allow me to live. It is not your way."

He needed her to answer a disturbing question. "Did you have anything to do with the tampering of the sleep circuits, that caused us to orbit this planet for ten years?"

Tammy looked surprised, and then bowed her head, "Does it matter? I will take the blame for all the wrong on this expedition."

"It does matter. You are still young, and you've been conditioned to think the way you do. Your actions may not be entirely your fault," explained Al.

"I do not think your trial will find me innocent."

"No," Al said honestly, "It looks like you might have caused the death of a twelve-year-old child, and endangered many more people. There will be those that want someone punished. If you didn't tamper with the sleep circuits, I don't believe death will be the price."

Tammy seemed confused, "I have been told you killed those you labeled terrorists with great fanfare, showing your justice to the world as warnings to the other *Earth First* members."

"You can't always believe everything you hear. You have to use your head."

He thought for a second and asked, "Have you been visited by someone that just wanted to talk?"

"Miss Emily has been by several times, and she likes to talk. She is always asking questions about things I don't want to discuss. She seems nice. Is she a psychiatrist?"

"She is your friend Tammy. Remember that because she can help you. Are you ready to go? We're kind of on a schedule."

His officers unlocked the jail door, fastened the restraints, and escorted her to the shuttle. Al followed thoughtfully behind them.

****

AL CLARK HAD A HOMECOMING party to attend. It was also a party to celebrate Chris's eighteenth birthday, and the first time he and his friends had been able to get together since coming to Camelot. Most of them lived in single unit habitat modules, so they met at the almost finished community center.

Made from large native timbers and Dura-Steel, the octagonal construction was a building large enough to hold nearly all the colonists at the same time. The center was *so* large that its conical roof, when completed, would furnish enough rainwater to last for weeks. It was a lot more room than the small group needed, but it was available, and it was empty.

Al and Chris met on the path and walked there together. They joined Ana and Kayla outside the entrance, and as a group walked in together. They found Robot Nine waiting patiently. He had prepared a large round table and loaded it with food and drink. Lit with LED work lights, it was a surreal setting in the center of the dark auditorium. Al thought it fitting to have a large round table in Camelot's village hall.

Elizabeth's footsteps echoed off the walls as she entered the room. "I hear there's a party here. Somebody pass me a drink; I think I deserve it."

"Rough day Mom?" asked Chris.

"I still think I deserve a drink even if it wasn't that bad."

Her son saw an opportunity and said, "You *do* realize that I too have been working real hard...and it's my birthday. I think I deserve a drink too."

"Well, I don't know...you think he's old enough Al?"

"Maybe a drink or two will quench his curiosity," He suggested.

Chris grabbed a glass and exclaimed, "All right—let's party!"

When Cody arrived the group was complete, and they ate, drank, talked, and just relaxed. It was a pleasant gathering, long delayed, that reminded Al of the importance of friends. Sometime during the evening, Al decided he needed to tell them his secret.

He had been considering telling them for some time, and this party seemed the perfect opportunity. There may not be another chance where they were all gathered together in a private setting anytime soon. Every one of them had asked questions about his mysterious surgery, and—he was tired of lying.

"I have found out something you should know," Al declared, "I'm a human being...in a robotic body."

Silence took the room, and his friends peered at him as if he had gone crazy. Their faces showed them wondering what kind of joke this was. When he did not smile, they began to think he might not be kidding. Al told them everything, including details even Cody and Robot Nine did not know.

"I have learned I was the victim of an accident that left me without the use of my arms and legs. They offered me a chance to participate in an experiment, where they would place my brain in a robotic body and then make me a member of the *Excalibur* expedition—and apparently, I took it.

"I was brought aboard at the last minute, to be the secret backup alarm to awaken everyone upon arrival at Avalon—which obviously failed. Someone tampered with both the computer revival systems and my specially designed hibernation pod, leaving us orbiting the planet until—believe it or not—a meteoroid landed in my head.

His friends were still speechless, and could only stare in disbelief.

"The tiny meteoroid seems to have taken my memories, but it woke me up and saved us all from being a ship of ghosts. The emergency operation I had was to remove the meteoroid that was causing me some additional problems."

Another piece of information they might find amusing occurred to him, "My name is *not* Al Clark. The roboticist's assistants liked to call me 'Alarm Clock' as an inside joke and placed the label on my door. When I woke up, the label was so old, all I could get from it was Al Clark. Funny...huh?"

When he finished, his friends did not move or speak for several additional seconds. Cody lowered his head, and Robot Nine refilled the ice buckets. Cody was not sure if Al's revealing himself was a good idea. Never the less, he decided to back Al no matter what happened.

"Is that how you were able to get from one side of the camp to the other in a matter of minutes?" Liz asked.

"Yes."

"And the fire in the power room?"

"I don't seem to need a lot of air. To tell the truth, it was not that hard."

"Are you like...superhuman?" Chris wanted to know.

"I certainly don't think so. For the time being my body is only slightly better than ordinary human beings."

Al's revelation was still sinking in for Ana and Kayla, who were completely taken by surprise. Kayla picked up on how he began his last question and wanted it explained.

"Why do you say for the time being?"

"Because I have another mode. An enhanced mode."

"What are you like in enhanced mode?" pressed Ana.

"I don't know. I haven't tried it yet."

"Why not?" asked Chris.

"I'm not sure I'm ready yet."

Liz thought about all they'd been through together. "How come you haven't told us before now?"

"I only recently found out myself, and I wasn't sure you were ready."

Al explained his need to tell Doctor Cody after the attack returning from the native's caves. He told them how the roboticist Doctor Florida became involved, and how Robot Nine knew all along.

Chris asked the robot, "Why didn't you say something?"

"No one ever asked, sir. If someone were to ask, I would be required to answer. I am pleased no one did because I did not want to cause Chief Clark any trouble."

The party was becoming too sober for an eighteenth birthday celebration, so Al laughed and said, "O...kay, now you are all members of my secret society. I need all of you to help me figure out this craziness. How about we call it the Al Clark secret society and everyone has to take an oath of silence. All in favor, say, 'aye."

One by one they acknowledged their vows until it came to Robot Nine. "I will not reveal your secret if no one asks. That is the best I can do, sir."

They laughed and toasted the pact, then tried to act as if nothing had changed; although it had. None of them would ever look at Al in the same way again.

****

THE TRIAL WAS SLATED to begin in two weeks, and psychiatrist Emily Saxton was still trying to understand her patient. The girl claimed to know nothing of the disabling of the hiber-pod revival circuits. Unfortunately, she admitted to sabotaging the ship after her revival. Tammy believed she sacrificed everything to stop them from inhabiting Avalon. Doctor Saxton saw the hidden doubts; uncertainties Tammy could not recognize.

They sat at the table in Tammy's makeshift jail. Emily was trying to get her to open up.

"Your foster parents were part of the *Earth First* group?"

"As long as I can remember they were. They were very proud of it."

"How old are you?"

"I'll be eighteen in December. Merry Christmas to me."

"It must be nice to be born around Christmas."

"My parents didn't celebrate Christmas...or my birthday. They said Christmas was a pagan holiday, and I did not deserve a party to celebrate my birth."

Emily frowned and answered, "That is entirely wrong. Everyone should be allowed to enjoy Christmas in their own way...you mean you've never had a birthday party?"

"I have them for myself. I give myself chocolate. Happy Birthday!"

"Would you like a birthday party?"

"I used to when I was little. It doesn't matter anyway; I won't live to see another birthday."

"And you won't with that attitude. You should try to be more positive."

"I can't. It's never worked for me before."

"If we can win this trial, your life could be much better."

"I would like to believe you. The more I think about it, the more I don't want to die."

Emily's evaluation stopped when Al walked into the room. He closed the door and joined them at the table. Addressing Emily, he said, "Can we talk outside for a minute?"

She followed him outside where he asked, "Well, is she crazy?"

"Depends on your definition of crazy Mister Clark."

"Is she sane enough to stand trial?"

"I think so if we can get her adoptive parents out of her head. They are the ghosts she lives with. She was highly radicalized to their beliefs."

"Is there a chance she can change?"

"Maybe in time...if we can keep her alive," stressed the psychiatrist.

Al frowned and confessed, "I have to admit, Emily, I think putting people to death is not the best way to start a colony on an alien world—it's against our best interests."

AL CLARK

****

CHRIS' MIND WAS NOT on the trial. He was working to complete his duties at the village power plant, hoping to make some excuse to get up to the ship and talk to the roboticist. Chris was intrigued, and contemplating the potential capabilities of Al Clark made him even more curious. A human mind in a robot's body?

How fast can he go...really?

How strong are his legs? Can he jump like the Hulk, the angry comic book hero? The more he considered Al's revelation, the more respect he had for his friend. Chris could not imagine the things that must have been going through Al's mind since waking up in that box.

Are his eyes capable of infrared? Can he zoom in on distant objects? Can he bend steel with his bare hands?

The questions were driving him insane, and he didn't want to bother the security chief. However, he knew Doctor Florida had the manual—the book of Al, and that the good doctor probably knew more about Al than Al did.

His mother noticed Chris acting oddly, as mothers do, and suspected he was up to something. She sat him down, and they talked. It didn't take long before he was spilling his guts.

"So you want to talk to the roboticist? Hey...I happen to need someone to bring down some supplies from the ship. Would you like to volunteer?" Liz suggested.

Her son smiled and replied, "I would be happy to get your supplies for you, mother."

"You can on one condition. You have to tell me everything Doctor Florida says. I want a full report."

Mother and son, in league together, for the betterment of Al.

Chris caught a ride with the morning shuttle and arrived outside the robot shop just before lunch time. He opened the door and walked in to find the scientist sitting at a table looking thoughtful. Music was playing in the background that he recognized as an old song, recorded before his time. The doctor appeared to be just the way Al described; an older man, short, with wild hair and a relaxed attitude.

"Are you Doctor Florida?" Chris guessed.

"Hi, son. You must be Al's friend Chris, am I right?"

"Yes sir, I'm Al's friend. If you don't mind, I have a couple questions for you."

Edward smiled and said, "Only a couple?"

Chris looked a little guilty and continued, "Al told us his incredible secret. A human with a robotic body and I do have some questions. The first one is, what music are you listening to?"

Edward Florida reached over and turned the music down, "Oh...that. I have a fondness for Beatles music. They were a four man group from the nineteen sixties. I like other groups from that era, but they are my favorite. They made a song for every mood."

"I thought they sounded familiar. Anyway, what do you think of our friend Al?"

Doctor Florida had considered this question. It would, in the future, be a question he expected to be asked again and again.

"Al Clark is a remarkable person with unique capabilities. He can do a lot to help protect us on this dangerous planet...and I like him."

"Um...what is he exactly?"

This question involved the scientist's field, and it was one he'd been contemplating since before he started his career, so his answer was simple.

"Our friend is a cybernetic construct. A human brain with complete control of a very sophisticated transport machine. He has a titanium chassis, made mobile by class five motors and actuators. His skin is a remarkable Tru-Skin covering that can heal itself, and his power pack will last for twenty years. I didn't even know this was possible."

"Who was he really...before the accident?"

"I don't know. There is no mention of his name in the book, only references to a subject fourteen. According to the book, the volunteer was educated, intelligent, and active before the accident. The book does not give a name to that person.

Chris asked another question. "He told us he has a second mode, what's that like?"

"Everything changes when he is in enhanced mode. I don't yet understand all of what the notebook implies. However, the changes are substantial. Doctor Hawthorn, the man that designed his body, was a genius. He was way ahead of his time and the leading expert on integration between the human brain and highly adaptive robotics."

"Do you know what Al is capable of?"

"That's the thing. The book only makes estimates. There wasn't time for many tests before they put him into hibernation for the trip. Nobody knows what he is ultimately capable of."

An idea had been germinating in Chris's head that might give them a chance to help Al find out what his enhanced mode offered. "Don't you think we should run some tests?"

"That is an excellent idea Chris, but how? I don't have the equipment to test him properly."

"What does it take to change his mode?"

"He must be on board to change it permanently, although Doctor Hawthorn did not recommend changing from normal to enhanced mode until the colony fully accepted Al." Edward hesitated, and continued, "There is an override, though. It's a temporary override, triggered by a phrase, which I believe lasts about an hour."

"Can we do the basic tests here, like hand and leg strength?"

"My tests would be limited. This place is not equipped to handle something like Al."

It occurred to the scientist that he had just referred to Al as a thing and that he would have to be more careful in the future how he referred to his friend.

Chris suggested, maybe a little too eagerly, "We could run some monitored tests down on the planet, maybe time some runs, or break some branches. What do you think?"

"Once again, we have to remember the consequences of his powers being discovered. We will have to do all our testing in complete secrecy."

"How about we take a shuttle to another part of the planet? I know just who can pilot it. It would be you, me, Al, and the captain. I'll be the coach. What do you think?"

"Wait a minute son; we'll have to talk this over with Captain Effinger and Mister Clark. I'll tell you what, you talk to Al, and I'll talk to the captain. Then we'll all get together and discuss the possibilities. How about that?"

Edward's suggestion was close to what Chris was hoping. *A field trip to put a Superman through his paces.* His friend being the Superman.

Chapter Seventeen

They landed just after dawn; after sneaking away from Camelot in the dark. The captain picked them up on the outskirts of the settlement shortly before dawn and spirited them away to test Al's potential in private. He flew them to an isolated spot with giant trees, rolling hills, rushing water, and plenty of open ground.

As discussed, the party consisted of Chris, Al, the roboticist Edward Florida, and the captain. When Al informed the rest of his conspirators, they had all wanted to come. With regret, to minimize suspicion, he had to tell them, "Not this time. We have to be discreet." They were disappointed but understood the risk. The group was small for a good reason.

Al was ready to get started. "Okay—how do you want to do this?"

Edward explained, "Slowly and carefully Al. Chris has devised a series of tests with my recommendations, starting with your legs and working from there. These will be informal tests that will give us a general idea as to your capabilities. We can refine them as we go. For this series of trials, I will be the record keeper."

Tobias Effinger, as captain, felt he needed to say something to the group. He retrieved some folding chairs from the shuttle and urged everyone to sit down.

"Slow and careful are the key words here. I don't want anyone getting hurt because we rushed things. Remember this is a potentially dangerous experiment, and I want all of you to remain cautious, especially you Al. Please—take your time."

"I'll do my best, Tobias. After all, I'm the one most likely to get hurt. You can count on it."

The robot specialist moved his chair directly in front of Al and looked him in the eyes as he spoke, "There is a phrase I will say to you. You will repeat the phrase exactly as I say it, and you will begin to feel a transition. Give yourself a few minutes to get used to the change before you try and stand up. I believe your enhanced mode will take some getting used to."

Edward looked around and silently asked permission to proceed. When the others nodded their approval, he asked his friend, "Are you ready?"

Al said, "Doc, I've been waiting for this since I found out what I am. Yes...I am ready."

"I want you to understand something. The time you spend in enhanced mode will subtract significantly from the lifespan of your body's power-pack. The twenty-year span is based on being in *human* mode only. When it gets depleted to a certain point, it will have to be replaced. Hopefully, by then I will be able to build a new one. Is that acceptable?"

"Come on Doc, let's get on with it. Oh, wait, what if I can't handle it? What if it's too much for my puny human brain?"

"You are controlling a very sophisticated computer that in turn controls your body. It can recognize high levels of stress and immediately take you back to human mode. It is one of the many fail-safes built into the system...um, your body."

Al was resolute. He had to know. "All right, let's do this."

Edward smiled and said, "All right, sit perfectly still. Here is the phrase: The metal of a man is measured by what is inside."

"The metal of a man is measured by what is inside," Al repeated.

No human being had experienced what Al now went through. The feeling of power steadily ramped up until it was ringing in his ears. Something changed, and the ringing went away. Everything he saw became crystal clear for a moment and then exploded into a blinding light. Then the light went out, and so did he. Chris had to reach over and grab him to prevent Al from falling out of the chair.

Thirty minutes later Al woke up and asked, "What just happened?"

Chris was the first to answer, "Tobias says the transition was more than you could process, and you passed out. How do you feel?"

Al looked around, "Well, I think I'm okay...my head is a little fuzzy. Otherwise, I think I'm good."

"I don't believe you were ready," Edward said, "You were too nervous, and you need to be relaxed. Maybe even close your eyes until everything else boots up. Do you want to try again?"

"Yes...how about we give it a minute—okay?"

An hour after Al passed out he tried again. This time, he cleared his mind and sat perfectly still with his eyes closed, and the transition was less traumatic. The power ramped up much as before, and when the ringing went away this time, Al could hear as he had never heard before. He quickly discovered he could tone it down and make the overwhelming input of sound more bearable. For a moment he just sat there; adjusting.

Chris started the timer about the time Al opened his eyes. For a half second, his eyes struggled to focus, and then everything became clear. There were small, discreet indicators on both sides of his vision providing essential readings of power, temperature, and distance. In-between the information tell-tales was the sharpest, brightest, and most detailed world Al had ever seen. He found that if he focused on a particular spot and concentrated, he could zoom in and out at will.

"I can hear you now," the captain pointed out.

The sounds the mechanisms inside him made were indeed slightly louder. He slowly stood up, hearing each motor and feeling each actuator react to his commands.

"Man...this is unbelievable. I can see better, hear better, and it feels great! Let's do some testing."

He took three steps forward and fell on his butt as his legs ran out from under him.

Chris helped him up. "Maybe you have to lean into it or something...you think?"

"Ha! Now why didn't I think of that?" Al brushed himself off and laughed at the same time. He had a good feeling about this. "What's the first test?"

In a large flat area nearby, Chris marked off forty-six meters (fifty yards) for a track and placed a marker at both ends. The captain stationed himself at the far end, and Chris stood by the starting point with Al. Edward prepared his data pad to record the occasion.

Al staggered to the far marker the first time and then walked on the way back. Each consecutive trip became a little faster until he thought he was ready for the clock.

He felt so good he decided to test his new ability unrestrained, and picked a tree in the distance, waved at his friends, and took off running towards it. His enhanced eyesight allowed him to see every rock or branch in his path, and he was there and back before anyone had time to complain. He was *extremely* fast and already enjoying his newfound freedom immensely.

The fifty-yard dash he did in a little over four seconds. Almost a second faster than the fastest human ever recorded.

"Now we have to see if you can jump," suggested Chris.

As it turned out, Al was also good at propelling himself upward. When he tried hard, he could clear thirty feet straight up. It wasn't long before he figured out he needed to bend his legs when landing. He left dents in the soft soil and almost fell.

He was amazed how much was visible from thirty feet up, and he jumped three and then four times, each time looking a different direction. On his fourth leap, he spotted something move behind the shuttle. A flash of gold caught his attention where gold should not be. Something was watching them from the other side of the aircraft.

Al motioned to get down and pointed to the rear of the shuttle. Chris and Edward ran for cover while the captain took two steps to his left and picked up the rifle from where he left it; pointing it in the direction Al indicated.

The cat-like animal sensed something wrong, and came around the shuttle at a full charge, pouncing for the closest victim—the short, wild-haired roboticist. Unfortunately for the beast, it was not fast enough.

Al didn't take the time to think, he reacted by knocking the creature out of mid-air, and threw it twenty feet into the open. It took the captain a second to realize what had happened, but he quickly gathered himself, aimed, and shot the thing several times with the laser.

"We should have checked this place better when we got here. Let's have a look around now," suggested Al. "To make sure we don't have more visitors." He reminded himself once again. *Never let your guard down.*

After a thorough search of the surrounding area, Captain Effinger stood staring at the large white cat and its golden stripes, with the rifle nestled in one arm. "It looks like a saber-tooth tiger, except with white and gold fur. Look at the teeth on that thing. I'll bet it weighs at least a hundred pounds!"

Chris said, "I wouldn't want to run into that thing anywhere without a rifle...by the way, nice shot, and thank you. It was headed for me next, umm...after he finished with Doctor Florida."

The captain looked at Chris. He then shook his head and replied, "Don't thank me, thank Al. If he hadn't been here, Edward would probably be dead. If I couldn't get a shot off fast enough, maybe you too."

"I am really happy, Al, that you are my friend and not my enemy," exclaimed Chris. Al just grinned while the rest silently agreed.

At precisely one hour into his first foray in enhanced mode, a timer somewhere wound down, and he became *normal* again.

Well, as normal as he could be. Al could feel the power slipping away, and he noted again how good it felt. He wanted it back.

On the way back to the settlement, Edward chuckled and said, "Dr. Hawthorn even spelled it m-e-t-a-l, instead of m-e-t-t-l-e, in the phrase we used to take you to enhanced mode. He was a genius with a sense of humor. Incredible."

****

ANA TRIED IMAGINING what it would be like to run like the wind and jump thirty feet into the air. There would be no sprained muscles or stomach aches or any of the myriad other things associated with being human. To never have your body grow old.

"What was it like, Al...in enhanced mode?"

"It's hard to describe," Al answered. "You know how sometimes you wake up refreshed and rested, with every fiber of your being telling you to get up and do something? It's kind of like that—only times ten."

It was beginning to get dark, and they had gathered at Elizabeth's place. When Chris moved out to a place of his own, she was allowed to keep the double sized quarters they had. Rank does have its privileges.

"How do you like having a place of your own Chris?" asked Al.

"Oh, it's great. Nobody is bugging me to do this or do that...no offense Mom." Chris couldn't help but laugh, and they all joined in.

"Seriously though, it is nice to have my own stuff in my own place, and...it's so much quieter." Chris was enjoying his new freedom, and could not resist kidding his mother.

His first friends in the new world watched a beautiful sunset, and afterward, they retired inside to eat—and to talk. It was early evening, and the original six: Chris, Liz, Ana, Kayla, Cody, and Al, gathered for support.

The conversation turned to Tammy Shoemaker's trial. Al asked, "What do you think will happen at the trial this weekend?" He had visited the prisoner several times and found himself feeling sorry for her. She seemed more and more to be a victim of circumstance.

Liz had doubts about whether or not Tammy Shoemaker would be allowed to live.

"There are people here that want her head put on a stake and placed at the gate. I heard some say we should stone her. It will be a tough fight for the defense."

Al pointed out, "I hope the jury realizes that we are already down to eight hundred and thirty people. For a healthy community, I think the more people—the better."

Chris appeared uncomfortable and did not join the speculation.

To change the subject, Doc Cody asked Al, "Have there been any more sightings of the dinosaurs...the Riktors?"

"Actually no. Nobody's seen anything but a few tracks around here in a while. Although, we did find a pair of smaller ones pulling rocks from the entrance to the Sansi caves during one of the Watcher's rounds. The man on duty made the Watcher drone visible and tapped them on the head a couple of times. They ran away, and the natives could be heard cheering from inside their caves."

"Do you think the beasts have learned their lesson about attacking us?" asked Chris.

Al thought for a second, "I would like to think so, but I don't believe it. It would be wise to keep our guard up. I have four armed men continually circling the compound, the two Watchers a little further out, and Robot Nine roaming all over. I think we're as safe as we can be."

Around the village, Al had seen the visitor from the caves following behind Rahul and Cindy, "How is the native doing? The Sansi girl?"

"She is a bundle of sunshine," replied Ana. "Everywhere Kira goes she leaves people smiling, and people love talking to her. She's due to head home soon and tell her tribe of her time with us. How I'd love to be a fly on the cave wall when she does."

"She asked me how the little people can live in the radios. She is a riot," Chris added.

It was one of the better evenings. An evening that one remembered as *pleasant* later in life. They talked, and made wisecracks, and laughed. They all tried hard to hide their fears and be hopeful for the future

****

KIRA WAS READY TO LEAVE. She missed her home, and then again she did not. She was torn between leaving these wonderful people and going back to her loved ones; all the time thinking she might not be allowed to return to this magical village. She believed the gods were happy with her, and hoped they would allow her to return. The problem was that someone else from her tribe deserved a turn.

The wonder of the things she saw while living with them made her feel grateful. The ones called Cindy and Rahul were kind and helpful. They showed her everything she asked about, and some she did not.

There are rain rooms inside their homes where they can clean themselves, she was thinking, *and soft rocks that bubble in the waterfalls to make dirt disappear.*

She was allowed up to their starship and given a slow, well-explained tour of the Excalibur only two days ago, and the images were fresh in her mind.

Her beautiful blue home slowly circled below her, while she held tight to the rail; afraid of falling. The captain explained why the Sansi could see the ship as it passed overhead at night. When Cindy tried to explain the hiber-pods, she could not imagine sleeping for so many years. She, like many others, loved the habitat hub where you could fly. There were many wonders, and their explanations were only partly successful. Even without fully understanding, she loved it all.

They showed her the medical center, where it was possible for the gods to heal themselves. When she learned a god could die, it confused her for awhile. The idea took some time to sink in. She was, however, a smart girl, and eventually accepted the possibility.

Cindy, Rahul, and a god that carried a stick that shot fire accompanied her to the caves. As soon as they were close enough to see her home, they were greeted by what must have been most of the Sansi tribe.

The natives were so excited and glad to see them they were all talking at once. Members of the tribe brought baskets of fruit out and laid them before their guests as a tribute to their saviors.

The two contact specialists and the girl had come a long way in their ability to communicate. Regardless of their progress, the humans still could not keep up with the rapid-fire conversation going on between Kira and her tribe.

Cindy turned to the girl and asked, "What are they talking about Kira?"

"They say to me...that you have saved them."

Puzzled, Rahul asked, "What did we do?"

"You made the Riktors run away with your magic floating rocks that cannot be seen. My people are very...happy."

The contact specialists enjoyed the party regardless of the fact they had no idea what the natives were talking about. After a while, they figured out enough to know that somebody had neglected to keep them informed about matters concerning the natives. Someone should have told them the Sansi had been attacked.

Kira was glad to be home. She missed her family and friends and the simple, familiar life that led. Most of all she missed Toji, her special friend that would someday become her mate.

The things that she had learned while with the Kuthra told her that the gods were in many ways very much like the Sansi. The gods that came to save them were smart and powerful, but they were not *all*-powerful. The Kuthra, like her people, could be killed. As the party of three gods left the Sansi, her people raised their right hands above their heads as a sign of farewell. Watching them leave, Kira was thinking, *not only are they strong and powerful—they are brave.*

****

SITTING IN HER PRISON, Tammy Shoemaker was scared and angry. Angry that she was afraid. Her parents told her many times that giving yourself to your cause would lead to a place in heaven. A beautiful place where you would live forever. Lately, though, she was beginning to have doubts.

Her prison was a standard habitat module, placed as far away as possible from the rest of the settlement with bars added to the windows. A ten-foot chain link fence with barbed wire on top surrounded the habitat; leaving a fifteen-foot walkway all around. She was allowed thirty minutes a day to spend in the *Yard*, which she learned to treasure.

Most of the time she was alone inside her cell, with her guard stationed in the yard. The captain stopped by once, the big cheese security man twice, her lawyer and psychiatrist switched hours every other day. Christopher Morris, to her delight, was seeing her more and more.

He surprised her two weeks ago when the guard knocked on her door declaring she had a visitor. Standing outside was Chris, with a lot of questions, most of which she had answered numerous times. At first he appeared self-righteous and patronizing. As time went by, Chris kept coming back, and she began to think that he might care what happens to her. He was always so thoughtful, and supportive, that Tammy thought of him as her ray of hope.

Her life on the *Excalibur* had been a solitary one. She purposely made no friends, afraid they would ask too many questions, so there was no one to talk her out of her destructive tendencies. She had effected her sabotage in the belief she was helping her cause. Looking back now, she realized she left her cause behind a long time ago. Never again would she hear the stern teachings of her stepparents, or set foot on the polluted, over-populated Earth. During her incarceration, she had time to think and began to realize her parents had been wrong on many matters. In Tammy's eyes—she had played the part of a puppet and a fool.

Chris was sitting across from her at the table when she asked, "Do you really think they'll let me live?"

"They can't...execute you. You have too much to offer the colony. With your skills, there must be a hundred jobs you could do."

"The colonists will not believe I am sorry. If I were them, I wouldn't either."

"I believe you're sorry, and I'll tell them that. I know a lot of people that will testify the same way."

"The people you refer to are maybe a dozen out of eight hundred and something. I find it hard to be optimistic after what I've done. To most of these people, I am a murderer at the very least. Maybe I deserve to die."

Chris reached over and took her hand, "Listen to me—there are a lot of good people here that just want to live their lives. They work hard and try to be fair to each other. I think you'll find more forgiveness in them than you expect."

He turned her hand over and took on a scholarly attitude. He looked down at her palm and said, "You have a long life line...that ends in three children...and a lot of laundry to do. I see dishes...and robots—lots of robots."

A smile grew on the girl's face. "You don't know anything about palm reading. How could you possibly make those predictions? You are crazy."

"Crazy huh? We'll have to wait and see, won't we? But I'm pretty sure I got the robot part right."

Chapter Eighteen

Al knew he needed sleep. It was a fundamental part of being human. He was thankful it was only about four hours a night, instead of the average eight for most people. He could tell when he needed sleep by a lack of concentration and a frustrating fuzziness in his head. Still, he hated to waste time sleeping.

The morning of the trial he woke from the dream at two in the morning, straining to understand the meaning behind it. He was so close this time. His rest only lasted a few hours, and he lay there wide awake, wishing that sleep would retake him so he could finish the dream. After a while, he realized it was hopeless—he was awake, and the dream was gone. Al got up, dressed, and left his little habitat house to check on the men in the security shack.

It was a beautiful summer evening with a cloudless sky that allowed a million stars to light the surface of Avalon. As he walked the path to the security shack, the night air helped to calm his nerves.

Al was *not* looking forward to this day of the trial. The security arrangements were in place, and everyone's place assigned. Regardless, there were so many concerns to worry over that he thought it might be a good idea to get a jump on things. For reasons he could not quite put his finger on—he felt apprehensive.

Upon entering the security shack, he was met by Robot Nine and two of his men, all three staring at monitor pads and the images transmitted by the Watchers. The robot was in a corner cubicle re-charging himself and had something he wished to report.

"Sir...Watcher number two detected a large Riktor just outside the fence ten minutes and fourteen seconds ago."

Al frowned and replied, "Not what I wanted to hear first thing this morning, Robot Nine."

The robot beeped and said. "I am sorry, Al Clark."

Of all the days for a Riktor sighting, this was not the day he wanted to have this happen. They had seen no activity from the creatures in almost three weeks and were beginning to believe the village was relatively safe.

"Is he still there?"

His senior officer, Sid, answered before the little robot had a chance to reply, "No Chief, he looked around a little bit and then left. It was a bit scary there for a minute, though—it was close to the prisoner's quarters."

Al knew there was a risk involved with placing her so far out, but he had to isolate her from the rest of the colonists. When someone does something as serious as she did, it was best to keep them as far away from the victims as possible. He wanted to keep her safe long enough to have a trial.

Al asked the robot, "Robot Nine, how long before you're finished re-charging?"

"I require another hour and twenty-one minutes sir."

The chief also knew there would be pre-trial preparations going on in the prisoner's quarters, "How many people are there at the jail?"

Sid replied, "The lawyer, the psychiatrist, your young friend, the guard...and the prisoner, of course."

"Is Chris there?"

"Been there all night, sir."

What has gotten into that kid?

"All right," Al said, "You guys stay here and have one of the Watchers remain at the fence line where it was spotted. I'm going out and take a look around."

Chris had been seeing a lot of Tammy Shoemaker lately. Al was aware of his growing interest, and it worried him. It seemed Chris was getting attached to someone who may or may not be a good person. There was also the possibility of her execution. If that were to happen, it could change how Chris viewed life forever.

In the dim early morning light, the jail compound appeared ominous as he walked up to the gate. The crude prison was remote and sitting in the middle of open space resembling a small fort. The ten-foot electrical fence, topped with barbed wire, and the bright lighting caused the prison to appear quite capable of keeping people in and monsters out.

The guard, a specially picked colonist familiar with security protocol saw Al coming and opened the gate.

"Did you see the Riktor a little while ago?" Al asked.

"I don't know about any Riktors sir, but I saw a ten-foot dinosaur. It was like looking at a history book. I've never seen a real one...it about scared me out of my boots. One minute he was there at the perimeter fence—and the next—it was not."

This man apparently did not know the Sansi name for the creatures.

"What was he doing?"

"He was just looking around—real quiet like. It seemed interested in the two posts it was standing by. As I said, I only saw him for thirty seconds or so."

"How close did he get to the fence?"

"Oh...about ten feet, sir."

"Sid will be out here in about an hour. He'll be responsible for getting the prisoner to the trial with your help. In the meantime, keep your eyes peeled and remember trouble can come from any side of this facility. All right?"

The man acknowledged the order and Al continued inside to check on Tammy and her guests.

Al entered and tried to keep the tone light. "You guys are having a party, and you didn't invite me?"

"It's not much of a party. We're not very good at it." Chris replied without humor.

It didn't look much like a party either, with everyone sitting around looking worried. Scattered around the table were lists of prospective witnesses and ledgers of all the people on Avalon. It didn't look good for the defense.

"Hey—come on people—this is no way to win a trial," admonished Al, "I don't know a lot about courtroom procedures, but it seems to me that you need to think positive. Show them Tammy is not a threat, and that she could be of help to the colony. If you can manage that, you'll be halfway to winning. Stress Tammy's skills and talents, and concentrate on the crazy beliefs her parents drilled into her since childhood.

She admits she is guilty; you only need to prove she was coerced into doing what she did."

Chris turned to Tammy with a told-you-so look on his face.

"Such as it is, that is our plan," admitted Tammy's lawyer, "I hope you are part of the jury...that would help a lot."

Al regretfully informed them, "My name won't be on any of the twelve pieces of paper they pick out of the hat. Because I'm security, I am exempt. Think positive, though; all you need is seven people that don't believe in capital punishment, out of the almost eight hundred names in that rather large hat. The odds are in your favor."

"That's what I've been trying to tell her," Chris said.

"You're just going to have to have faith in the general goodness of human nature," suggested Al. "Can I talk to you for a minute...outside, Chris?"

Chris followed him outside, and Al informed him of the Riktor sighting. He looked Chris square in the eyes and told him, "I want you to stay alert on your way to the auditorium, and stay close to officer Sal and the guard. Whatever you do, don't forget that many threats are facing Miss Shoemaker today. If you have to stay with her—please be careful—okay?"

Al left thinking he could do little to discourage him from seeing the girl. Young love can be like a bulldozer and almost unstoppable. But it concerned him that Chris appeared to be falling for a girl that may not live long enough to see her eighteenth birthday.

AL CLARK

****

AS AL HEADED BACK TO the security shack, scattered clouds crept across the sky, diffusing the starlight and creating eerie shadows that crept across the landscape. He was thinking of the unfortunate girl and what she would be facing this day, and if there was anything more he could do to act in her defense. He decided he must speak for her at her tribunal. Al didn't believe an eye for an eye would do the community any good. She was so young, and he wanted her to have the chance to prove that her life mattered.

It was eight o'clock in the morning, and Al had arranged a meeting at the shack to go over security for the trial. All his men except Sal were there along with Robot Nine. Sal was responsible for the prisoner and would deliver her to the auditorium at the start of the trial.

"I do not understand Chief Clark, the proceedings you are preparing are illogical," stated Robot Nine.

Standing by the door, the security chief asked, "Why do you say that robot?"

"You left Earth to come here and make a new beginning. Logic tells me that you will need every person, and more, to live on this planet safely. Why would you choose to kill one of your own?"

The settlement of Avalon was turning into a bittersweet journey and was proving much harder than imagined. Still, Al believed its beauty and compatibility with human needs made it worthy of the struggle.

"That, my friend, is what I'm hoping the defense can get across to the jury."

Al stood up and issued assignments. "Robot Nine, I want you circling the fence perimeter exclusively." Al gestured to the four officers on the left side of the room and continued, "You four will join him and post yourselves so you can see in all directions and the rest of you men...and women, will be stationed inside the auditorium. I'll fill you in on individual posts once we get inside."

The trial took place in the community center auditorium at ten in the morning. The now completed center, located in the very middle of Camelot, was something the colonists were understandably proud of. All sidewalks crossed the wide path surrounding the building, making it truly the center of the community. Its steeply angled roof peaked at almost one-hundred feet tall, with the entire surface used to collect rainwater. The roof overhang also provided for a wrap-around porch that gave people a place to get out of sun and rain.

The building was designed and used as a multi-function facility, with rooms that circled the interior walls that included school rooms, several stores, a clinic, and even a small church. The large open space in the middle was for community gatherings. In the back of the building was a shuttle pad large enough for all four shuttles.

By nine thirty the auditorium was packed. Bleachers lined the outer walls of the room, with the prosecution and defense tables, the jury box, and a judicial bench for the captain placed in the center. The sounds of the crowd echoed through the large open room; buzzing with anticipation.

Sal brought the prisoner in at nine-fifty and sat her next to her lawyer at the defense table. Another officer stayed with her while Sid joined the audience. The captain entered, sat down at the judge's table, and at precisely ten o'clock called the proceedings to order. He did not wish to prolong this procedure, so he minced no words.

"Tammy Shoemaker is charged with sabotage and murder. How do you plead?"

Tammy's lawyer stood up and declared, "My client wishes to plead guilty...with extenuating circumstances."

Captain Effinger showed no signs of surprise. He had expected as much. "All right then, let's get started. Please draw the names of the jurors."

A young boy pulled twelve slips from the hopper, and the names were called out. One by one, seven women and five men were sworn in and seated in the jury box. That done, the prosecution called his first witness, and the trial began.

The murdered girl's parents were called to testify; the psychiatrist, the doctor that did the autopsy, water quality experts, and the few people that knew Tammy were all requested to say their piece. They discussed the power room fire, the hangar door malfunction, and of course, the poisoning of the water. The prosecution attempted to make her appear evil while the defense framed her as a victim of a form of brainwashing, and could not be held responsible. The whole time, Tammy sat there with a blank look on her face, as if she couldn't believe this was happening.

When all the witnesses had testified, and the character references heard, the captain asked, "Is there anyone else that would like to speak?"

Al raised his hand, "I would like to say something, Captain."

"All right...go ahead Mister Clark."

What Al had to say was this, "I just want to point out that we are setting a precedent here. If she is found guilty and executed, we will be following the path that believes taking the life of a criminal is a deterrent to serious crime. You should know that there is no evidence to support this conclusion. I don't believe she is a danger to the settlement, and she sincerely wants to make amends for her actions."

Al paused for a second, to allow the jury time to think about what he had said, "There is also the issue concerning the number of people necessary to colonize a planet. A lot of brilliant people got together and decided that one-thousand individuals is a good number to start a colony. We are down to eight hundred and thirty colonists, which in my book, is pushing the limits. We need every person we can get to make this settlement a success. We can't afford to kill her."

Captain Effinger frowned at Al, so he finished with, "That's all I have to say."

The rain started around two o'clock. A slow, steady rain that could be heard tapping on the roof while the jury listened to the testimonies. The captain recognized Tammy and asked her, "Do you have anything to say. Would you like to come and be heard?"

She hesitantly said, "Yes...I would."

Tammy stood up and moved to the center of the room.

"Most of my life they told me that the colony ships are war vessels sent out to conquer new planets. They are loaded with Earth's elite and wealthy and use biological weapons to wipe the world clean of native people to make the planet suitable for occupation. My parents made me believe what they said was the truth. I now believe I was being deceived."

Tammy knew that what she said next could make the difference between life and death. She composed herself and continued, "I am very sorry for what I've done. I thought I was earning my way to heaven, but I was making myself a place in hell. Please—I want to live—so I can do what I can to help this colony survive and grow."

The defense and prosecution made their closing statements, and the jury retired to one of the classrooms to deliberate. Tammy's fate was now in the hands of the jury.

Sunset came, and the rain got harder, and louder. So loud, in fact, that it began to get hard to hear inside the courtroom. Al retreated from the noise and stepped outside onto the porch to await the verdict.

The Watchers were excellent surveillance tools, with only a few limitations. The Riktors were a species of cold-blooded dinosaur, and the drone's night vision had trouble tracking an animal that took on the heat signatures of its surroundings. The added restriction that the high-tech drones could see little in a downpour compounded the problem. It was pitch black and raining cats and dogs, and the Watchers were pretty much useless.

"There is a break in the fence," Robot Nine reported, "Multiple tracks leading to the confinement facility. I am pursuing."

A silent alarm went off in Al's head to match the screeching from his pocket. He pulled out his pad and said, "I need to know how many there are and where. Report quickly Robot Nine; we don't have much time."

Al had considered this scenario. Unfortunately, it didn't include the rain. He turned and ran back into the building yelling into his communicator, "Everybody inside! You officers outside round everybody up and get inside quickly."

He stopped in front of the captain and yelled over the rain, "Can you fly in this Tobias?"

His friend replied confidently, "Son—I can fly in anything—what is it you need?"

"Follow me. I'll explain once we are in the shuttle."

They made their way to the back, exited the building, and ran to the nearest shuttle. The captain worked the door lock in record time, and they climbed in. Sixty seconds after receiving the alarm and Al was closing the shuttle door to the pouring rain.

"They have split up, sir," the robot's voice reported, "The tracks indicate at least four...possibly more. The intruders appear to be headed for the community center. I am following the tracks of two reptiles moving to the east side of the settlement. Be advised; I am having trouble navigating the soft ground, and my forward velocities have decreased considerably."

Al realized the situation was quickly becoming serious.

"Tobias, can you see well enough to stay fifteen feet off the ground?"

"We may not be able to see what's directly below us, but I can use the instruments to keep us at whatever height you want," replied the captain.

"I need you to say the phrase to enhance my abilities. It seems I can't make it work alone. Believe me; I have tried."

"What do we do then?"

"You're gonna fly over them, and then I'm gonna shoot-em."

The captain trusted Al's judgment, and he didn't have any better ideas. His simple reply was a rising, "O...kay."

He started the shuttle while Al grabbed the two rifles he had stashed under a seat—just in case. He was determined not to be caught unprepared again.

"Are you ready Mister Clark?"

"Ready as I'll ever be...I guess."

Tobias spoke the phrase: "The metal of a man is judged by what is inside."

For the second time, Al repeated the phrase and felt his systems ramp up. The feeling of power filled his senses, his hearing rose sharply and then settled down, and his sight became equivalent to the eyes of an eagle. Once again, he was an enhanced human.

Tobias asked, "Are you all right, Al?"

"I have never felt so right. Let's go and find us some dinosaurs."

Al threw the shuttle door open, and the captain lifted off, swerving in the direction of the marauding predators. Al wrapped his leg around a pole and leaned out of the opening in the aircraft to find a target for his rifle.

"Can you see anything Captain?" Al yelled.

"I can see enough. Something is going on ahead—be ready."

Something flashed by under the shuttle, and the captain performed the sweetest one-eighty that Al had ever seen. Five seconds later, Al was above a full-sized adult Riktor running full-tilt towards the community center, with the shuttle only feet above its head.

From his vantage point, it was an easy shot. He fired three times as fast as the rifle would allow and the creature fell hard; disappearing in the mist behind them.

Captain Effinger was one with his machine, and the amazing little craft did everything he asked of it. Tobias used his instruments and data pad to find them, while Al shot the beasts from above. The pouring rain with the almost silent shuttle flying above made them easy targets. They didn't even know what hit them.

The third beast caught on, though, and stopped his rampage to watch the spacecraft fly over his head. Al reminded himself these were not stupid creatures. Al motioned for the captain to lower the shuttle, and he jumped six feet to the ground. The Riktor was livid, and when it advanced on him he shot it several times in the head, and it went down for the final time. The captain brought the shuttle back down; Al jumped in, and they went looking for more targets.

The next Riktor had a quarry of its own. A man and woman tried to make it to the community center and were caught by one of the enraged predators when Al and the captain came on the distressing scene. It was too late for the unfortunate colonists, but the captain and Al still had to deal with the murderous animal.

This time Al didn't wait until the captain lowered the shuttle. As they flew over, he dropped his rifle into the shuttle and jumped on top of the rampaging animal. While he rode the beast's neck, he pulled the always handy pistol from its holster—and shot it at close range. Al had to jump to keep from being crushed by its fall.

The captain picked up the blood splattered Al, and they resumed their hunt once again. There was nothing he could do for the two people who had given their lives to Avalon.

The fifth beast surprised them. It must have heard or seen his fellows fall, and overcome with rage, he hunkered down and jumped, grabbing the landing skid of the aircraft. The shuttle leaned so far over that Al slid out the door and fell to the ground fifteen feet below. Either by miracle or advanced technology, Al managed to land on his feet, roll, and bounce back up to run after the departing shuttle.

With the rain pounding on his head, and his feet slipping in the mud, he realized he could not catch up. Al could not help. Fortunately, the captain had an idea of his own. He slowly took the shuttle and the creature straight up forty feet or so and stopped. The shuttle was listing badly and was almost sideways under the weight of the beast when Al saw the captain lean out the door and shoot it. The animal screamed, let go, and fell to the muddy ground below, which caused the shuttle to roll almost all the way around until the gyroscopes could get it level again. After a moment, the captain popped his head out the pilot's window, smiled, and gave the 'Okay' symbol.

They had taken out five adult intruders. Al thought, *the beasts were trying to wipe us out and came in force.*

Then he remembered that Riktors hunted in pairs. *There was at least one more.*

****

THE CREATURES SEEMED determined to make it to the human gathering place, and that is where they found what they hoped was the last assailant. When they landed, the massive wooden doors to the community center were splintered and laying on the floor just inside the auditorium. Standing at the hole in the wall was the back of a powerful creature advancing on two people in the middle of the room. He could not use his rifle. The community gathering place was full of people huddling at the top of the bleachers.

When Al stepped to the side, he realized the beast was threatening Chris and Tammy. Some idiot had handcuffed her to the table, and Chris was doing all he could to pull the table—and Tammy—away from the beast. Al realized, *I need to get it outside where I can deal with it.*

He decided that keeping his secret was secondary to saving his friend and the girl. The decision caused him to run up to the monster from behind—and kick it. With feeling. Hard enough to leave a good size wound in the Riktors leg with the intent of getting its attention and luring it back through the door. It looked around to see what had assaulted it and promptly knocked Al into the bleachers with a flip of its tail.

Al untangled himself from the wreckage of the bleacher seats and began screaming and yelling at the Riktor over the sound of the rain. He headed for the door with the thundering beast right behind him. On his way by, a quick thinking Officer Sid tossed Al his rifle, replacing the one Al dropped on his flight to the bleachers. It was an excellent throw, and it probably saved Al's life.

Once outside, it was a simple matter of rolling to face the opposite direction and shooting the beast in the head several times before it had time to tear his head off. The creature fell into the mud with a final scream—and died too close for comfort. The apex predator was never threatened by death and died with a distinct look of puzzlement.

Al, covered in mud and dripping with blood, took a moment to collect himself. He walked back through the broken doorway into the auditorium and told his men to pair up and search the entire compound for more intruders and check for casualties.

They had managed to survive the worst attack yet. The only problem was that this time—everyone in the auditorium knew that Al Clark was not normal.

****

THE FIRST THING AL did was go over and shake Sid's hand. He told him, "That was some throw, Sid. If I ever need someone to watch my back, you'll be at the top of my list."

Officer Sid looked down and smiled, "I didn't take the time to think about it, it just happened—but I'm glad it worked. You did way more than I could have and better than any...*person,* I've ever seen. Don't worry, sir, no matter what happens I've got your back.

"Thank you, Sid, I appreciate that. I might need all the friends I can find after this."

Other than a few cuts on Tammy's wrist from the stupid handcuffs, she and Chris were okay. Robot Nine was found lying in the mud with his arms broken, a significant dent in his body, and he was repeating, "Sorry...sorry," over and over.

No one in the auditorium was injured, save for cuts and bruises from scrambling up the bleachers. A man and a woman were found just outside, slain as they tried to get to the community center. It was something Al and the captain would have to learn to accept. Other than that, the colony had survived relatively unscathed.

Now that the danger was over, the rain reduced itself to a soft drizzle. Fate changed direction and allowed the tension to drain from the atmosphere.

"Who handcuffed her to the table?" Al wanted to know.

The man assigned to stay with her during the trial answered hesitantly, "I did sir...I wanted to make sure she didn't make a break for it."

This reply increased Al's anger, and he growled at the man, "Where is she going to go? We are in the middle of nowhere and on a dinosaur infested planet for goodness sake."

"I'm sorry sir, I didn't think."

"You're damn right you didn't think. I didn't ask for you to handcuff her—you should have asked me first. Do you realize you almost caused the deaths of two people because of your lack of judgment?"

The man was obviously embarrassed and regretful. He replied, "Yes sir, I do...and they would have been killed if not for you, sir. I still can't believe you stopped it."

Al, feeling it best to postpone any further conversation; turned and walked away.

It was starting to register with the crowd that something extraordinary had happened right before their eyes, and questions were forming in their minds. People were standing around murmuring to each other, trying to make sense of these extraordinary developments.

A man yelled out, addressing his question at Al, "How did you do that? You put your foot into that animal and then ran faster than it did to get outside. How is that possible?"

Someone else joined in, "How *did* you do that?"

From somewhere in the back of the crowd, a voice was heard. "He can't be human. He must be one of those..."

Captain Effinger saw that things were getting out of hand. He stood at the judge's table, held up his hands, and said in a commanding voice, "Everybody! I think we've had enough excitement for one night. The threat is over, and it is late. We will have to finish the trial in a day or two. Go home and get some sleep. We'll reconvene and finish this after we clean-up and make the camp safe again. All senior staff, I need to speak with you now. Everyone else is to go home."

Al gathered with his men, told half of them to go home, and ordered the remaining half to stand watch until morning. The captain assembled with the senior staff and gave the necessary orders to have the Riktors disposed of, to repair the fence, and to begin repairs to the damage caused by the attack.

When Al finally had time, he cleaned himself up as best he could and went to find Chris and Tammy sitting at the defense table, patiently waiting until someone could escort the prisoner back to her cage. By this time the community center was almost empty.

Al walked up and said, "Come on you two, I'll walk you home."

They were the last to leave and didn't bother closing the door.

"Are you two okay?" Al asked as they walked out to the jail.

Tammy answered, "Never mind us. How are you doing? You must have flown forty feet and then landed in the bleachers. That had to hurt!"

"It wasn't as bad as it must have looked. I'm all right. The bleachers broke my fall," Al said. While he tried to make light of the conflict he gave a discreet warning glance to Chris. Maybe he could still get away with saying it was an adrenaline rush, or maybe people would settle down and decide, with all the excitement, they had seen things they couldn't possibly have seen.

Tammy looked up and asked, "Do you mind if I ask a question, Mister Clark?"

"No, I don't mind—go ahead."

"I was there, not ten feet away from its open mouth...and then it was gone. It was right in front of me, and then seconds later you were shooting it in the courtyard. How *did* you do that?"

Her question made him see that keeping his secret would prove next to impossible. The colonists were smart people, and it dawned on Al that he would not fool them for long.

"It's a long story, Miss Shoemaker, but yes. I'm not an ordinary guy. I'm a human in a robotic body."

"You're a robot? Isn't that like...bad?"

Al thought for a second, smiled a little, and replied, "Not from where I'm standing."

Chapter Nineteen

Kira knew that something was very wrong. She awoke from her bed to the sound of screaming people and the roar of monsters in the distance. The first person she woke was Toji, and in a breathless voice she told him, "The Riktors are attacking the Kuthra!"

Still half asleep, he listened for a moment and asked, "Is that coming from their village?"

"Yes," she said, "I think our friends are in trouble. The Riktors sound very angry."

"What should we do?"

"We must try to help them.

"*Can* we help them?"

If we gather enough Sansi, we can.

Their decision made, they woke the elders first, they in turn woke the rest of the cave dwellers. A group of twelve strong warriors was assembled, and armed with their best spears and knives. Then they rushed to aid their gods, with Kira and Toji in the lead.

It was a long time ago that her people had fought a Riktor. Toji's grandfather had brought one down many years ago, but it had cost the life of four Sansi. The tanned hide from the beast was all they received as reward. Their philosophy since then, had always been that it was better to hide than to fight. It was now time to change their thinking and do what they could to assist their saviors from the stars.

The rain diminished to a light drizzle while they made their way through the dark forest in the quick and silent style learned from their ancestors. Kira had been outside after dark only a few times in her life, and she found it quite disconcerting. The cloud cover and rain made it especially dark, and it was hard to see where they were stepping as the group moved as fast as they could, with only the redeeming advantage of youth in their favor.

The lights of the place *where they kept the bad Kuthras* came into view. Because of the angry roar they heard as they approached the compound, they were not surprised when lights were blocked by the silhouette of a towering monster. Outside the line of magic sticks that protected the gods, the taller than ten-foot beast paced back and forth, becoming more and more agitated as it listened to the destruction of his pack.

The warriors were resolute. They circled to both sides where the lights helped to reveal their prey and began throwing their spears, aiming to get as close as they could to something vital. Jumping and yelling they stayed just outside the creature's reach and launched their stone-pointed spears with an accuracy that surprised even them.

The Riktor they fought was a large elder creature, with a roar that shook the trees nearby. His tail thrashed and slapped the ground within inches of the always moving warriors. The Sansi were nimble, and their tactics relentless, harassing the beast and generating enough fear that it retreated into the human settlement to escape. It crossed the downed section of the fence and headed into Camelot—towards the jail.

****

AL RECEIVED AN ALARM from Watcher One, with images that were distorted and grainy. He was beginning to think the drone had malfunctioned when the raging dinosaur burst into the light of the prison gate, followed by the harassing natives.

Al's enhancements had worn off hours ago, and with all the excitement and exertions of the previous attacks, he was not at his best. He was so surprised and slow in his response that before he could pull his sidearm, the beast was screaming in their faces.

The Sansi were all around it and still driving their spears into its blood stained hide when it did something strange. It spun around and appeared to plead with its attackers. Its spinning stopped as it faced the three humans, and Al thought he detected a look of confusion cross its face. He shook his massive head, trying to clear the growing lethargy from his mind. The Riktor was dying, and it didn't understand, even as it fell, that the fight was lost.

The Sansi had succeeded in their attempt to stop the last remaining monster, and it fell to the ground with a crash not ten feet from the three overwhelmed humans. Chris, Tammy, and Al owed the Sansi their lives, and the natives were more than happy—they were ecstatic, and jumped up and down yelling like the children they were not long ago.

Chapter Twenty

A l convinced Kira that the beast they killed must be the last of the creatures and thanked them all for their bravery. The jubilant Sansi bowed to the people they thought of as gods and headed home to begin telling the tale that would go down in Sansi history as one of their finest moments.

Chris, Al, and Tammy were exhausted. With the stress of the trial, and then almost losing her life, Tammy wanted only to lay down in her bed and sleep, so the two men led her into the habitat jail and said good night; leaving her in the care of her guards.

On their way back to the village, Chris wanted to know all about Al's experience.

"How did it feel to be enhanced again? Did you find out anything new?"

"I have to tell you, Chris, it's like nothing you can imagine. It makes me feel like I can do anything. I had to be careful after the attack, that I didn't accidentally hurt someone until it wore off."

"Did you learn anything new?"

Al smiled at the memory of the feeling. "It seems I can see pretty well in pouring rain—in the dark. My legs can survive a fifteen-foot drop—with no ill effects, and my foot is a lethal weapon."

"Yeah, I'll have to remember not to ask you to kick me...if I do something stupid."

They walked for a while, both deep in thought. Chris remembered the look on Tammy's face, as she watched Al assault the monster and lead it outside. He remembered the entire village watching.

"Do you think this is going to cause you trouble?"

"Up until I went into the auditorium to get what I thought was the last creature, I think no one would have been the wiser. Now, with all that happened, I'll have some explaining to do."

"So...what *are* you going to do?"

"At this point, Chris, I have no idea. I have a feeling when everybody gathers together to finish this trial; the village will be judging two people—Tammy Shoemaker and Al Clark.

****

THINGS WERE DIFFERENT for Al after that night. People walking on the same sidewalk as he would turn and go the other way. He would sit down at a table in the cafeteria, and people would appear uncomfortable, and move to a different table. The colonists that weren't afraid of him had a thousand questions, and he grew tired of trying to explain himself. He began to throw himself into his work. He gathered his men, and told them his entire story, leaving nothing out. They assured him they were there for him and would do what they could to make his life a little easier.

The one thing that didn't change was the support from his real friends. They gathered to discuss his situation the night after the attack, to let him know they would do everything they could to persuade the colonists that Al was not a threat to the colony, but an asset.

Elizabeth Morris converted her two habitats, placed end to end, into a comfortable place to live—or visit. She kept the onboard parts printers busy on the *Excalibur* producing window shades, louvered cabinets, dishes, and numerous other home furnishings. Cloth curtains framed each window, ready to be closed when the sun became annoying, and as most women seem to enjoy having pillows about, there were plenty to go around.

"I'll sit with you when you go to breakfast...if you want?" volunteered Liz, "Actually, I like that idea. That way they'll know I'm on your side."

"That is an excellent idea," Ana said in agreement. "How about we all join you. We should probably get together for all our meals. We can't have you eating alone."

Kayla, Cody, and the captain agreed. Chris was at the jail keeping Tammy company.

Liz confessed with a hint of a smile, "I was hoping to have a nice quiet breakfast, just Al and I."

Cody laughed and said with his Haitian accent, "Now Elizabeth, there will be plenty of time for that once we convince the good people of Camelot that Al Clark is not a bad man and someone to fear."

They made arrangements to meet for breakfast, and eventually, everyone said their goodbyes and left to go to their homes—except for Liz and Al, who were left sitting side-by-side on a love seat.

"I was serious about having breakfast; just you and me. I like you, Al—as a person. I would love to get to know that person better."

"You're going to make me blush."

"Can you...blush I mean?"

"I don't think so, but it sure feels like I should be."

They sat for a while unsure of what to say, until Al volunteered, "I like you too Liz, and I have been wanting to spend more time with you." A crooked smile greeted her glance.

Before things got too awkward, Al stood up and said, "Umm...I need to get going. I've got to get up early." He was quickly becoming uncomfortable, and he knew it showed. Nevertheless, he gave her a peck on the cheek before he made his way out the door.

****

THEY LEARNED THE CRAFTY beasts had dislodged a large boulder and sent it careening down a hill, rolled over a fence post, and opened the electronic fence for their invasion. It required almost a week to accomplish the repairs brought about by the rampaging creatures. To bury the Riktor carcasses alone required two days, and the replacement of the fence added to that total. The colony took the time to mourn and bury the unlucky couple that died seeking safety, and the Camelot cemetery grew a little larger.

Seven days after the attack of the Riktors, the villagers gathered and brought the long anticipated trial to a conclusion, with a somewhat anti-climactic ending.

Tammy Shoemaker was found guilty.

It was determined she had willfully sabotaged their ship, threatening all their lives and had to be made accountable. However, the testimony given by the defense gave the jury pause about recommending capital punishment, and after much discussion, she was sentenced to live a life of community service. Which ironically is what all the colonists agreed to when they joined the expedition. In her case, though, she would wear an ankle bracelet to record her movements, and assist anyone that had need of her skills. She would be free; with restrictions.

Even after Tammy was escorted out, to be fitted for her anklet, the settlers continued to sit in the bleachers. There was another issue they wanted addressed, and they seemed reluctant to leave until their leaders addressed their questions. Chris stayed behind, feeling something serious was about to happen.

Al could hear the whispers and the muted discussions of the crowd as they worked up the nerve to speak aloud. Finally, one gentleman stood up, raised his voice, and asked the question uppermost on the settlers' minds.

"Mister Clark...are you human?"

This question had haunted Al a lot lately, and he was glad to finally be able to bare his soul, "Yes sir, I am a human being—fitted with a robotic body."

"Isn't that another way of saying *cyborg*?" a woman yelled.

The term Cyborg promoted fear. Science fiction dramas always depicted them as killers and destroyers. The combination of man and machine is usually portrayed as an experiment gone wrong; creating man-made monsters.

"I don't think of myself as a cyborg. I guess, by some definitions, I might be considered one. I really don't know. I think of myself as a human with a prosthetic body."

"Have you ever hurt anybody...even accidentally?" she pressed.

Al decided it was time. Somehow, he needed to make them understand he had their best interests at heart. He simplified his situation for everyone by telling them his life's story—the parts he knew at least. He started with his rude awakening, and for thirty minutes was given their undivided attention.

Al ended his confession with the dispatching of the dinosaur they all witnessed. He explained his strengths as *somewhat* better than normal, and why he believed it necessary to keep his abilities secret. For his own safety, he made no mention of his dual-mode system or the fact that his power-pack was limited.

When he finished speaking, the building was so quiet you could have heard a nail drop on a dirt floor. It was a lot of information to process, and the silence lasted for a good minute or two.

Chris picked this opportunity to defend his friend, "Chief Al Clark is one of my closest friends, and I would trust my life to him. As a matter of fact—I have. He has always come through for me. If I were ever in trouble, he would be the first person I'd turn to."

One by one his friends stood up and expressed their feelings for Al. How they trusted him to know the right thing to do and the fact that he was a good man with extraordinary abilities. Chris, Ana, Kayla, Liz, Doctor Cody, Doctor Florida, and a few others had their share of good things to say. Robot Nine assured them, "You have nothing to fear from Al Clark."

When they completed their statements, the captain took his turn.

"Mister Clark was an experiment that went right. I'm sure that Doctor Hawthorne, his creator—if he were alive—would consider Al's transformation a complete success. As an officer, I have never worked with better. As a person, I consider him a trusted friend. The people fortunate enough to call him friend—are lucky indeed."

Captain Effinger thought for a few seconds, took a deep breath, and added, "We all come from a world full of prejudice that has stunted human growth for thousands of years. Here, I believed we had gotten past all that and could treat each other with respect as equals. Al is here, he is one-of-a-kind, and we should thank our lucky stars that he is the man he is. If not for him, there is a good chance we would *all* be dead. Keep that in mind as you pass judgment on him."

Al Clark felt pretty good when he left that crowded meetinghouse, surrounded by his friends. They shielded him from the many questions and protected him from the few that were still openly hostile. A man can also be judged by the strength of his friends.

Things got slowly better after that. He felt more at home. He had no secrets, and he had the added benefit of friends he could trust to stand by him. How much more can a man want?

****

THE MONTHS PASSED, and Camelot became a village. There was much to do, and the colonists learned to work together. The Sansi wanted to repay the Kuthra for saving them from the Riktors—and brought Kira as a sacrifice; which the gods graciously declined. Their mercy made Kira and her clan both grateful and relieved.

The natives confirmed that the Riktors in the immediate area had been wiped out, and until more moved their way, they were safe from the beasts. For the first time in their lives, the Sansi could go outside at night and no longer fear the wrath of their ancient nemesis.

With the help of Rahul and Cindy, the indigenous people were eventually convinced that the people they thought of as gods were not omnipotent. The Kuthra were as mortal as the Sansi. Nevertheless, the Sansi marveled at their new friend's intelligence, kindness, and mysterious technology. Their benefactors began teaching them and assisting with a limited number of improvements to their lives. One of the first miracles they received was a steel knife that could slice and cut almost without resistance.

The Earthlings could not dissuade the natives of Avalon from their belief that their ancient prophecy, foretold generations before, had come true. The Kuthra came from the stars to save them from the Riktors. This fact was one truth they would write into their journals for future generations.

Seeds from the seed bank on board the *Excalibur* were brought down and planted, and crops begun. Frozen embryos of farm stock, in unique hibernation pods of their own, were revived and eventually raised into cows, chickens, pigs, and sheep. While they waited for the livestock to get old enough to be useful, they hunted the local game.

The hunting was good, and the captain began to experiment with Avalonian wild game in an attempt to replicate a good old-fashioned hamburger. The laser rifles made it almost too easy. Still, the taste of a traditional burger eluded him.

The winter was harsh at times. The settlers expected this and were prepared, which allowed them to make it through without too much difficulty.

Doc Cody met someone. She was an agricultural engineer that proved to be a lovely woman with many of the same interests as he. They could be seen walking the perimeter late at night holding hands. He was black, and she was white. It bothered no one.

They threw a birthday party for Tammy with a little help from Chris and his friends that left her in tears. When Christmas day rolled around, they gave her so many presents she needed two people to help carry them home. Chris said she cried for an hour.

Chris and Tammy got married. It was a foregone conclusion when one saw how they looked at each other. Few were surprised when it was revealed they were expecting a child.

Ana and Kayla were spending a lot of time together and were the best of friends. Some even considered them a couple. Very few found it odd.

Doctor Florida laboriously repaired Robot Nine, and even equipped him with some enhancements. He now had three legs—to match his three arms—that he could deploy for navigating soft ground. Although the little kamikaze was not quite as fast, mud was no longer a problem. He also sported a painted on security uniform; complete with a deputy badge.

Elizabeth and Al moved in together, and although it was awkward at the beginning, they learned quickly to allow for each other's unique needs. It was a good relationship, and they were both quite happy. The colony had accepted him for what he was, and he was content.

The captain insisted on and organized a Thanksgiving celebration. Long tables were set up outside and covered with fruits and vegetables from the shipboard farm and the first produce of the first harvest. The Sansi brought their favorites. Fresh filtered water was available within arm's reach, along with a fair selection of wine from Earth and a small sampling of Avalonian wine. Everyone attended, and all had a good time.

For the first time, the Sansi were able to enjoy a beautiful starlit evening. Most of the natives had never had the opportunity to experience or appreciate a night life. Lanterns lit the outside of the community center and contributed to the atmosphere of celebration, while a small group of colonial musicians played softly on the center porch.

During the party, the natives were introduced to many kinds of Kuthra foods, and for the first time—the relaxing effects of wine. It turned out to be a hugely successful party and went much better than anyone could have hoped.

At midnight, the humans introduced the Sansi to the age-old human tradition of *The Toast*, when the captain initiated a mass salute where everyone took part.

As a single group, the Sansi and Kuthra clinked and raised their glasses, and loudly proclaimed—"To Avalon!"

Chapter Twenty-One

Standing at the top of a grass covered hill, with a sweet smelling breeze at his back, Al Clark reveled in the bright morning sunshine of a perfect spring day. Jagged heights filled the horizon as the sun hoisted itself up and kissed the mountain tops.

In the valley below, the small idyllic village of Camelot was shaking off the night and was well into the process of beginning a new day. The faraway villagers appeared to be enjoying the day as much as he.

Someone was running up the hill towards him yelling something—a couple of words over and over; maybe a name, maybe a warning? He cupped his ears with his hands to better hear what the person was saying, but the sounds came muffled and distorted; carried away by the wind.

The person got closer and closer, arms and legs pumping, and the words became clearer and clearer until there could be no mistake—It was Elizabeth, and she was yelling, "It's a boy! It's a boy! We are grandparents!" It was official. They were the proud grandparents of the first human child born on Avalon.

Al finally understood why the dream always made him feel—happy.

ABOUT THE AUTHOR

Jonathan G. Meyer was born and raised in the St. Louis area, and has been an avid reader throughout the course of his life. He is the middle child of a family with seven children, and because he was the odd child out, he spent many days alone with a book. All books can take you to new places, and he used them to travel to many. However, he ultimately prefers the worlds of Science Fiction. Sci-Fi has always been one of his passions.

The books he creates are a throwback to the cheap pulp paperbacks he bought as a teenager. Books that one could carry in a back pocket. They are adventures that portray nostalgia for the past, excitement for the present, and a fervent hope for the future.

Books by Jonathan G. Meyer

AL CLARK- Christopher's Journal (Prequel)
Al CLARK- (Book One)
AL CLARK- Avalon (Book Two)
AL CLARK- Thera (Book Three)
AL CLARK- Earth (Book Four)
Also available:
VINCENT- A Starship like no other.
A CURIOUS ORB- A Trip in Time.

AS AN INDEPENDENT AUTHOR, reviews are a vital component for success. Good reviews create exposure, and recognition of an author's efforts. Not-so-good reviews help them perfect their craft. <u>Please be kind and post a review wherever you purchased this book.</u>

Ingram Content Group UK Ltd.
Milton Keynes UK
UKHW020655240723
425668UK00013B/480